The Watermelon Kid

The Watermelon Kid

A Novel by Bill Terry

Louisiana State University Press
Baton Rouge and London
1984

Designer: Albert Crochet
Typeface: Linotron Trump Mediaeval

LIBRARY OF CONGRESS CATALOGING IN PUBLICATION DATA

Terry, Bill.
   The watermelon kid.

   I. Title
PS3570.E696W3   1984   813'.54   84-5730
ISBN 0-8071-1177-5

For Mary Lou, Matt and Cathy, and Linda

The Watermelon Kid

THE ROADHOUSE CIRCUIT

This story is about A. J. Poole and his friends to whom he was known as the Watermelon Kid, and it took place on the old roadhouse circuit, mainly in Arkansas, back in the 1950s along the river roads that ran into U.S. Highway 70 when it was fast and narrow and dangerous. You might say that A. J., his good friend Pierpont Higgins, and the members of the Highway 70 Six, the band A. J. helped form, were the pilgrims, and the salted-floor, sweat and howl roadhouses full of wild screamers from the fields were their Canterburies. If the crops were good, the boys who harvested them—the soybeans and rice and cotton—pulled into places like Flossie's and the Shake Loose Club and the Silver Moon to leave their money and sometimes their blood. They came with their girls or in search of them to dance on those salted floors under the glitter balls or to fight outside on the gravel parking lots. You could get a fight as easily as you could get a drink, and if you got hit by a chair in a brawl when you had been minding your own business, it was just one of those things. But those chairs didn't come apart the way they did when they hit old Hop-A-Long in the picture show; they were real cane bottom dandies and they could knock your head off. The people came to hear music, and the more like the sound of an air raid it was the more they appreciated it, and they drank up enough beer and whiskey and set-ups to wash a train.

This, then, is the story of all of them, of an interlude in our time when the country was young and noisy and a little wild. It could never happen again, at least not in the same way, and it's probably a good thing.

I

1

A. J. POOLE got the name the "Watermelon Kid" on a hot night on the White River at Batesville, Arkansas, back in 1947 when A. J. was seventeen. They raise a lot of melons in Arkansas, and in those days they held a festival every summer to celebrate the harvest. It was a two-day affair with bands and dances and boat rides, a fishing derby, and a watermelon queen. They also held a watermelon eating contest.

Later on, the thing became known as the "White River Water Carnival and Beauty Pageant," but it was just called "Watermelon Day" then, and the beauty pageant was nowhere near as important as the contest to see who could eat the most watermelon. The winning queen got a $35 gift certificate from Thorndike's department store while the eating champ got a boat or a new motor worth $100 anyway. And there was heavy betting on the watermelon eaters, but nobody bet on the queens.

Usually, the festival came in the middle or latter part of August because that was the hottest time of the year, but that summer it came on August 4. The reason was that on July 31 the temperature had got to 107 and when night fell it was still so hot the fireflies were dying and the stars looked red-eyed with the heat. On the first, it got up to 108, and it was so bad people were arrested for swimming naked or in their skivvies in the cool White River.

They couldn't have that, so Police Chief Bimbo Wilson and Mayor Billy Pierce decided to call the contest early to take people's minds off the heat and swimming naked. They brought the stands down to the river and announced on the radio that the festival would start on the third and that the watermelon eating contest would take place on the fourth at Tim Allbright's boat dock, starting promptly at six o'clock.

They couldn't have picked a better night for it, for the temperature had hit 109 at noon, 110 at three in the afternoon, and by six o'clock there wasn't any ice for twenty miles except for what the chief and Mayor Pierce had brought to cool down more than a hundred melons in Tim's minnow tanks.

By seven o'clock some of the best watermelon pickers and eaters in that part of the country were lying belly-up and groaning on the bank or had been carried home in someone's car. At 7:30, only A. J. and Jimmy Pickens, who had won the year before, were left and they were as wet as river moss and gagging like dogs on oysters. They had chewed, swallowed, and spat their way through six melons apiece and were going to eat seven if it killed them.

And it might have. But chief judge Pierce called it a draw just before eight when he saw that Jimmy's eyes had started to bulge and A. J.'s had begun to roll just like Billy had seen his grandfather's that day he had his stroke. The problem was what to do about the prize, a brand-new $120.00 Evinrude outboard motor. There was no way you could split up that motor. No way at all. The mayor didn't know what to do. He looked at the two boys who were leaning against the side of the dock wiping themselves with towels.

Said Mayor Pierce: "You boys want to flip for it?"

Jimmy shook his head. Jimmy was a big, hairy boy with narrow eyes who looked older than his eighteen years because of his hairiness and the Chinese eyes. He said his thinking was that since he was last year's champion and hadn't been beat, the prize was his.

"A champion has rights," Jimmy said.

"Maybe on that," the mayor said, but he wasn't sure. He addressed the two boys again and said how would they like for the people to vote on it.

Jimmy looked around at the crowd. He counted some eighteen or twenty uncles and aunts and cousins and he knew that most people who had bet had bet on him—the champion. Jimmy said "fine."

A. J. was a big boy, even then. He had thick brown hair and blue eyes that could be laughing at you and be sorry for you

3

at the same time. He was strong and square-backed, and that day he was wearing bluejeans and a blue shirt with a red bandanna around his throat. He shaved on Saturday nights.

All A. J. said was: "I can do without that motor."

"How's that?"

"Don't need it. Got one. Got several in fact. What I don't have and can use is the honor. That's right. The honor of being the co-winner of the White River Watermelon Eating Contest. Don't mind sharing it a bit. Jimmy Pickens can eat a lot of watermelon."

So Jimmy got the $120.00 Evinrude and A. J. shared the title. And when Mayor Pierce told the crowd what had happened, he shook A. J.'s hand and presented him as A. J. Poole, "the Watermelon Kid." The name stuck, and A. J. didn't mind, since his initials stood for Amber Jerome.

But nobody had won any money and so the gamblers weren't happy. Speed Washburn, most of all. Speed was a big-time gambler from Hot Springs. He always came up to Batesville for the watermelon eating contest and bet three or four hundred dollars. Sometimes five. Speed and some of the other gamblers got to A. J. and Jimmy, and Speed said:

"How long's it been since you boys went to the can?"

They told him about an hour.

"Then it shouldn't be long," Speed said. "Not after that much watermelon."

Everybody caught on.

"Hey! All right, Speed!" someone said.

"Fantastic!"

"That's good thinking, Speed."

They made their bets and drove in about twenty cars out to Socko Rawlings' place on Highway 167. Socko was the biggest gambler in Batesville. A. J. and Jimmy rode with Speed. Speed was driving his brand-new Oldsmobile and he hit every chuckhole and bump in the road. Both boys looked uncomfortable when they got to Socko's.

A lot of the guys had flasks, and Socko offered the others beer. They got up a poker game in the front room and laid a blanket on the dining room table to shoot craps. But those were just pastimes; the big money was on the two boys. Over $2,000.

At 9:15, Jimmy went out for a stroll on the front porch and everybody noticed how small his steps were. He didn't walk far. A. J. didn't move from the couch in the front room.

Speed kept asking them: "How do you feel, boys? How're you doing?"

"We're OK. Doing just fine."

At 9:30, Jimmy started to sweat. He leaned over and whispered to A. J. "How're you feeling, Kid?"

"Fine. Feeling no pain."

At 9:40, Jimmy began wringing his hands and his feet were dancing. And then at 9:47 precisely, Jimmy let out a little scream and bolted down the hall to the back of the house. It was all over.

After that, everybody drove down to the Silver Moon in Newport to hear Wadie Moses, the new country singer from Nashville, Tennessee. But they were all talking about the Watermelon Kid.

A. J. and his mother owned a boat dock on the White River at DeValls Bluff in Prairie County. They also owned and operated a catfish restaurant set up in an old streetcar with a sign out front that said "EAT." They sold hush puppies with the fish, and fries and all the raw onions you could eat.

But A. J. didn't care for work. It was not that he was lazy or unimaginative or without enterprise. Quite the contrary. But all of his energies, and they were considerable, were directed toward the avoidance of what you might call permanent labor, a thing he found totally irreconcilable with his restlessness.

I remember one time we were sitting in Benny McDermott's Fantail Club out on Highway 70 near Brinkley. Cookie Stafford was there and Benny. It was a hot Saturday afternoon and we were drinking Falstaff and eating Benny's popcorn and stuffing it in like hampsters when A. J. said:

"God dog, but wouldn't it be nice to take a little run down to Reynosa?"

"Where?" we said.

A. J. took out an Esso map and showed us where Reynosa, Mexico, was, just across the border from McAllen, Texas, 900 miles away. I told A. J. he was out of his mind and laughed. I was not quite through laughing when A. J. and Cookie went out the door and jumped into A. J.'s pickup, headed for points south. That's the way he was. He was working at the time on Wendell Ford's dragline on the Cache River making $10 a day—pretty good money for 1949—but he didn't give it a thought once he'd decided on a little run to Mexico.

And he paid Cookie's way—gas and enchiladas and whores. That was another thing about A. J. He was a generous guy, big-hearted and maybe a little foolish. As a result, he had a lot of friends. More than enough. Too many, maybe. Though I don't think he believed so. And it was a curious thing, the people A. J. knew and came into contact with seemed like they were always in some kind of trouble. I mentioned that to him once and he nodded, almost matter-of-factly, as if it was somehow meant to be that way. Of course, everyone has the inarguable right to select his own calamity, and most people do so quite capably, usually in search of something they can't or shouldn't have, but once in a while with a little help it can be avoided or at least mitigated. I think that was what A. J. Poole felt to be his responsibility. He never said so exactly, but he did have a knack for showing up at the scene of trouble, though the resolution of a given situation was often best forgotten, such is the nature of accidents.

A. J.'s mother was named Sally: Sally Wickersham, Poole, Dicus, Brogan, Lookadoo. Those were the names of her husbands, and she outlived them all. Wickersham and Brogan died in automobile wrecks from which Sally escaped without a scratch. Poole never woke up from a crop duster crash, and Dicus one day laid his head on a pillow and said, "Sally, I'm through," and he was.

She was faithful to the men she married, but in between she had one lover after another like a procession of summer storms. Some men avoided her because of her survival record while others were drawn like goats to a cottonseed wagon. When she married Jesse Lookadoo in 1946, she was fifty-six and he fifty and Sally said at the church: "Jess, I'm going to take good care of you. I've outlived my last husband."

Jess had smiled and patted her hand, but he didn't last fifteen minutes. He was still dressed for the wedding when he got hit by a Superior Forwarding freight as he came out of the old Hippolite Drug Store carrying Sally a Coke. After that, Sally swore off men completely, and she was depressed for quite a while.

Later that year, Sally pulled Jackson Lee Crawford out of the White River after his boat swamped in a heavy squall, and when Jackson Lee's ordeal was over, Sally looked happily up at the parting clouds and thanked God because she said she had just found a new calling. It was one which was to sustain her for a number of years and earn her the title of "the Florence Nightingale of the White River."

Now, the White River is fast and deep and nothing to fool around with. Men and women and boys and dogs and cows have been dying in it for years, and it has a population of dead equal to a fair-sized town. In one year alone, 1949, Sally pulled out nine fishermen, six duck hunters, two women, and three boys, and they all survived. But four others were gone before she could reach them and were swept away. The DeValls Bluff Chamber of Commerce gave Sally a plaque in 1950, the year A. J. went off to Korea, for services rendered to mankind, and during the ceremony, Wallace Bell, whom Sally had saved that past November, stood up in the audience and cried: "I'll tell you what: She's our own Florence Nightingale!" Chamber president Nub Thacker scowled at Wallace and said: "That will do!" but then he turned to Sally and smiled as he said: "But ain't that the truth?"

For the rest of her life, Sally did nothing else but sit down at the dock or cruise the river waiting for people to get into trouble. When A. J. came back from Korea in 1953, he helped Sally with her labor and personally saved four men from drowning before Christmas. On New Year's Day 1954 they presented A. J. with a plaque just like they had done for Sally. But that spring was a disaster. Between them, Sally and A. J. managed to haul out only seven victims and out of that number five were dead. It got to Sally.

A. J. came home one afternoon and he was surprised to find Sally in the kitchen instead of down at the dock. He noticed she had a pile of telephone books on the table and an even taller stack of newspapers on the floor. A. J. didn't think too much about it at the time, but as the weeks went by, Sally was there every afternoon and sometimes sat far into the night with her papers and telephone books, which came from nearly every town in the Grand Prairie: DeValls, Brinkley, Clarendon, Des Arc, Biscoe, DeWitt, Stuttgart, and even as far south as Gillett.

One night when Sally finally went to bed, A. J. sat down at the table trying to figure out what his mother was doing. It didn't take long once he realized that all the newspapers were opened to the obituary pages. Sally was checking the obits every day to see who had died. Then she'd look them up in the telephone books and write "deceased" by their names. A. J. found ten marked "deceased" on just one page of the Brinkley phone book. It was in the *p*'s.

After that, A. J. began to treat his mother with extreme kindness and compassion, for he felt she would not be around much longer. He was right.

Sally Lookadoo died on September 19, 1954. It happened about sundown on a warm day. Sally and A. J. were helping two fishermen from Little Rock come in with the boat. Sally tied up the bowline and gave a hand to the two men who lumbered up on the dock. A. J. took their strings of catfish and crappie and began cleaning them in the sink under the shed.

The river was smooth and low and the water made a lapping sound against the pilings of the bridge just downstream from the dock. A "cool" blew in off the water, a fresh sting of sweetness, and drifted through the shed and up the bank.

The next thing they knew a car came hurtling out over the water. It brought with it pieces of concrete and broken steel from the guardrail, and one of the tires sailed out and skipped across the river like a flat rock. The car flipped once and landed upside down in a backwater pool across the river from the dock. Pierpont Higgins, the driver of the car, said later that he was driving too fast.

Sally went into action. She pushed the two men out of the way and jumped in the boat. She pulled the cord and threw it in gear and was moving out of the slip when A. J. jumped in. The car had settled to the bottom of the pool and the four wheels minus one tire were sticking out of the water. Two of the wheels were still turning. There was no sign of the driver.

The two fishermen from Little Rock moved restlessly up and down the dock. They were excited and curious and frightened. One of the men looked helplessly at the up-turned car. He said:

"We ought to do something."

"What?"

"We can call somebody. An ambulance maybe."

The other man said no. "Come on. Let's get out of here. We haven't paid yet."

Sally cut the motor so they wouldn't ram the car and drifted in. She stood up, holding a rope with a life buoy. And then the next moment she fell over in the boat and didn't break her fall with her hands.

A. J. let out a cry and bent down to look at his mother. "What's the matter with you? Hey!"

And then he heard a noise from the car. He saw a head bob up from the driver's side with hands extending up, reaching for the chassis. The guy was trying to climb out of the window. His face came into view. His mouth was bloody.

The man said: "I don't want to die here."

A. J. addressed the man directly. "Look here," he said. "My mother just had a heart attack or something. Maybe it was a stroke." He looked at Sally. Her eyes were open and staring but she was breathing.

The man said: "I know how she feels. I am about drowned myself."

9

"You look it," A. J. told him. "But my mother there is in a bad way. She may be dying. I don't know if I've got time to pull you out."

"Well, can't you spare the time? I never learned to swim and I am not kidding."

Sally groaned. Her lips moved slightly and her last words were: "Save him, son. Don't worry about me."

"What did she say?" the man asked quickly.

"Hold tight," A. J. said and reached for the rope. Sally still had hold of it and he had to pry her fingers loose. "Now you take it easy," he told his mother. "I'm going to haul this sucker out and then I'm taking you to the hospital."

Sally died later that night without regaining consciousness. The next day, A. J. was pretty busy. Sally left a will saying she wanted to be cremated and have her ashes strewn over the White River. A. J. took his mother to Brinkley early that morning where the mortician, Floyd West, worked her in ahead of a pharmacist and bricklayer because of who she was. Sally was cremated in six minutes flat and A. J. was back in DeValls Bluff with her ashes before noon.

By that time, the house and the boat dock were full of mourners, friends, and former victims of river accidents who would not have been there if it hadn't been for Sally. Among those was Pierpont Higgins, who was still badly shaken from his accident. He had stayed at the house while A. J. was at the hospital.

A. J. sowed his mother's ashes over the White River at 3:30 P.M. on September the 20th, and the Rev. Harold Rooker presided at the services. Harold said the last words standing in the center of the bridge, and people were lined along the girders as the traffic went through. They even had a loudspeaker so the people could hear over the traffic. The eulogy lasted twenty-five minutes and there wasn't a dry eye in the crowd when Harold got through.

He told his listeners that Sally Lookadoo was loved by God because of her human kindness and generous soul. The reverend said that the grace of Almighty God had been manifested in the heart and body of Sally Lookadoo and that through her the Hand of Providence had reached out to snatch the weak, the strong, the rich, the poor, the old and the young, the smart and the crazy from a watery grave.

He opened his Bible and read from the thirty-first chapter of Proverbs:

"'She seeketh wool and flax, and worketh willingly with her hands; she is like the merchants' ship; she bringeth her food from afar. She riseth also while it is yet night, and giveth meat to her household, and a portion to her maidens. . . . Her candle goeth not out at night. . . . She stretcheth out her hand to the poor; yea, she reacheth forth her hands to the needy. . . . Many daughters have done virtuously, but thou excellest them all.'"

He added that Sally's spirit would live in the river forever and that as a token of appreciation, the people there ought to name that stretch of fast water below the bridge "Sally's Shoals" in honor of the woman "who died that others may live."

When he said that, the people clapped and cried at the same time.

Just before he finished, Harold spoke of men who would dedicate their lives to the salvation of others, disciples of the Lord who would show consideration for their fellow man the way the Good Samaritan showed us way back when. And then his eyes got hot and his tongue flashed. Mankind, he said, was heartless and cruel. Selfishness ran in men's veins and it was oh, so easy not to care about your neighbor. People were blind, he said, they were floundering and lost, they were on their way to hell and were sure to get there if they didn't change.

About that time a guy in a rowboat came floating downstream. He passed the upturned car and was getting ready to go under the bridge. The Rev. Rooker looked down upon him and scowled.

"Do you know where you're going, brother?"

The guy ducked a little and looked up. You could see the whites of his eyes.

"Crappie fishing?" he called back and shrugged. He didn't know what to say.

The reverend snapped his Bible shut. Then he closed with

a prayer in which he opened his eyes just once, when an East Texas Motor Freight truck whipped up his coattail, and the services at the bridge were over by four o'clock.

Sally's friends and relatives had brought enough food to supply an ocean liner between New York and Greece. There were hams and chickens and catfish and salads and potatoes and hot beans and maybe fifty loaves of bread, and A. J. iced down a couple of tubs of beer. The people lingered until about six when the beer ran out.

Bernice Sillicoe and her family were among the last to leave. Bernice said she spoke for all her family, which numbered sixteen, when she said: "You are in our prayers, Kid."

Then Marcie Pruitt came by. She had been waiting all day. She was wearing a tight, black dress with no sleeves. Marcie said: "I think funerals are just awful, don't you?" Then she stood close to him and said: "I'll be at the FrosTop this evenin' at ten and we'll go riding. If you don't think it's too soon after."

A. J. said he would see.

2

A. J. HADN'T had time to say much of anything to his house guest, but after everyone left, he looked in on Pierpont and found him in bed with the covers up around his neck.

"I'm sorry about your mother."

A. J. nodded and looked him over. Pierpont was not a big man and he didn't look very strong. His large round head had a bare spot directly on top and it was as smooth as a volleyball. His eyes were big and blue and looked very wise. His mouth was a bit crooked, slightly tilted, perhaps from too much worry. A. J. thought he looked like he worried a lot. His chin was round and a little sloped toward his neck and under it, hanging down like a root from an onion, was a stringy goatee.

A. J. said: "You're looking better."

"I feel better. It was quite an experience. Coming off that bridge and flipping over and hitting the water upside down, scared the devil out of me." He sat up straight in bed. "Look here," he said, "you saved my life. I've been sleeping in your house and we have yet to be introduced. I know your name is Poole and that they call you the Watermelon Kid. I am Pierpont Higgins from Ohio."

A. J. shook his hand. "What do you do, Pierpont?"

"I'm in tuna fish."

"Tuna, huh?"

"I represent a new company down in Texas. Clausen and Beatty. We are marketing a brand called Mermaid." Pierpont nodded sadly. "There are three hundred pounds of Mermaid tuna in five-ounce cans in the back seat of my car. I don't suppose I will ever see it again."

A. J. smiled. He liked this Yankee from Ohio. "Say. I've

13

got some Southern Comfort and there's some ice left. Want a drink?"

"Why, I would be delighted."

A. J. poured the whiskey and said: "In the morning we'll see about getting your car out of the river."

A. J. surfaced and shook the water out of his hair. He hung on to the side of the boat and told Pierpont: "It's a mess down there."

"What does it look like?"

"Tin cans all over the place. It's a wonder they didn't beat your brains out when you flipped over. I brought you some." He handed Pierpont a couple of cans.

"Oh, oh," Pierpont said.

"What's the matter?"

"The labels are gone. You cannot sell a canned product when the labels are gone!"

"I hadn't thought of that, but you're probably right."

Pierpont nodded and said: "You know, I think I am finished in the tuna business. With those labels gone, my loss is about a hundred and fifty dollars. I can take that. What I am coming to is I don't know how I will pay you for pulling my automobile out of the water."

"Don't worry about it. Take it easy. Look, I've got to run up to Lepanto in a couple of days. We owned a house up there and I'm going to sell it. You can come with me if you want to. Might do you some good."

A. J. borrowed Wendell Ford's tractor that afternoon and they pulled Pierpont's car and the cans of tuna out of the water and let it all dry out in the sunshine. The next morning A. J. checked in with Alvin Bates at the restaurant and told him to look after things for a couple of days. Alvin was the cook. He was black but smart. He had once told A. J.: "My old lady polished white women's silver for forty years and my old man poured cowshit on their front yards to make the grass green. Me I'm gonna go to town." Alvin drove two nights a week over to college in Pine Bluff. He was going to be a lawyer. He said not to worry.

A. J. climbed back into his green Chevrolet pickup and they drove on up to Lepanto.

It was a fine day for driving. The rice fields had turned gold, and the tall grain tossed and dodged in the wind and parted in rippling streams. Combines were working the rice, wading through like great paddle-wheel ships, and trucks were lined along the field roads waiting for the harvest. The soybean fields were still thick and lush, like miniature jungles, but the wind churned up the loamy soil under the beans and hurled it into the air. The smell of dust and ripening grain hung over the prairie.

A. J. looked over at Pierpont and grinned. "Whereabouts in Ohio?"

"Canton. But I have relatives in Arkansas. Oh, yes. In the town of Marshall. It's somewhere in the north central part of your state. I plan to go see them sometime. His name is Ned Wilson. Cousin Ned and his wife, Pearl. Ned is in the feed business and I understand is doing quite well. One day I would like to go into business for myself. I think I would do very well. I was educated at Ohio State University and studied business administration. I was named after the great Pierpont Morgan, the financier."

"Where'd you learn to drive?"

A. J. turned off Highway 70 at Forrest City and drove north on State Highway 1. They got to Lepanto about twelve, took care of business that afternoon, and around sunset A. J. pulled his pickup into the gravel parking lot at Flossie's Place.

Flossie's was a one-story, rectangular building shaped like a shirt box. It was painted pink and had black doors but no windows. An electric Schlitz beer sign was fixed to a pole in front and under this hung a shingle that said: FLOSSIE'S.

The music was already going strong when A. J. and Pierpont walked in and the people were howling. A. J. took Pierpont aside and said:

"If anyone gets smart with you, just tell 'em you're with me."

Pierpont looked worried. "I sure will."

Most of the people sat at little round tables not much wider than a toilet seat and in booths over on one side. The booths were all taken, as many as four people to a side in some of them. The bar stretched almost to the back wall, and it was full. The glitter ball was radiating out a little galaxy of shooting stars, and the band was hot and sweating. They were playing "I See Stars When You Kick Me, But I Can't Help Lovin' You." A few people were dancing.

Flossie was behind the bar. She was a big, broad-chested woman and loud as a siren. She saw A. J. when he came in and opened the bridge and pushed her way through the crowd. She was grinning like a donkey.

"Hiya, Kid. It's been too long." She gave him a shove. "Get over there and I'll buy you a beer."

Pierpont tagged along behind.

At the bar, Flossie pushed a scrawny teenager off the stool so A. J. could sit down. She lowered her eyes on the teenager like a queen does her vassal and said:

"Rex see your ID?"

The boy grinned and said: "Yeeeeees, m'am. You know it."

Flossie scowled. "Well, you take that beer and drink it where I can't see you."

"Yeeees, m'am!"

Flossie grinned at A. J. "So what's new, Kid? Pulled anybody out of the river this week?"

"Me," Pierpont spoke up.

"What's this?"

"Pierpont Higgins. He's in tuna fish."

"TUNA FISH?" She yelled it loud enough to be heard in Louisiana.

"He was. Lost his cans in the river."

Pierpont said: "The Kid pulled me out. He saved my life."

Flossie looked admiringly at A. J. "I remember once he got me out of a fix. It was night. Late. Raining like hell. Sounded like a tractor on the roof. My bouncer had gone home. Man showed up with a deer rifle. Cleaned my register and he was tying me to the piano. But the Kid was driving by and something made him stop. I saw him sneak in the side door. He picked up a chair and this bastard was still tying me up when the Kid put his lights out." Flossie roared with laughter. "It's good to see you, Kid."

The music had stopped. Flossie left to put some quarters in the juke.

Leroy Scroggins came through the crowd, twisting and angling like a garden snake. When he got close enough, he jumped on A. J.'s back and roared: "Goddammit, Kid! Where you been since Bed-check Charlie and the muck?" They were buddies from Korea. Leroy was from St. Joe, Arkansas.

"LEROY!"

They swung around in a little dance, and A. J. said: "How you been keeping? This your band?"

"These fartknockers? Naw, man. I'm wild carding it. Their piano player fell out with liver trouble. I'm just messing around."

"What happened, Leroy?"

"Well, to tell you the truth, I lost my band." He nodded. "Yeah. They cut out on me. Couple of months ago. Left me in West Memphis. And do you know that low-down Porter Seers stole my sax?"

"Naw!"

"Fuckin'-A. I'm gonna see him about that. If I can find him."

"You need to get you another band, Leroy."

"Yeah. Ought to. But I don't know. Got a bad reputation since I let 'em run out and get away with it. Maybe I've lost my touch."

"Not you, Leroy."

"Who's this?" Leroy said, looking at Pierpont.

A. J. introduced Pierpont and said: "He used to be in tuna fish."

"Oh."

The break was over and Leroy went back to the piano. Leroy played just about every instrument you would ever hear in a roadhouse or a nightclub. He'd bought his first guitar from the Square Deal Pawn Shop in North Little Rock when he was seventeen and a saxophone the following year.

(Not the one Porter stole—that was his third one.) He played them all: the sax, the clarinet, the trumpet, and he could handle the drums. But he liked the piano best.

Flossie was holding a table for A. J. and Pierpont next to the bandstand and waved them over. A couple of girls sat down with them and a guy A. J. knew from DeValls. One of the girls thought Pierpont's goatee was the cutest thing she had ever seen and kept twisting it into a point like an icepick and giggling. Pierpont was having a good time.

Spider Coombs was at the next table. Spider was a big fellow with a hard head, tiny eyes, and a neck as red as a stop sign. And Spider wasn't having a bit of fun. He had put away six or seven beers and a pint of Jim Beam and had sent Booger Elkins down the road to get another pint. Booger was taking his time, and Spider was getting tired of waiting. The top of the table was covered with paper balls stripped off the labels of Schlitz beer bottles. They were rolled up tiny and hard, like BBs. Spider had strong hands.

The music was going again, and Spider got up and walked over to the bandstand. He stopped below the singer and scowled up at him. The boy was picking his electric guitar and singing "I Met Her at the River but She Wouldn't Come Across." He didn't notice Spider until Spider stepped by him and unplugged his electric guitar. Then Spider bit the plug in his teeth.

Leroy said: "What the hell's going on here?"

The singer didn't say anything.

Spider said: "You talking to me, no account piano player?"

Leroy swallowed hard. He had a jagged face that looked like it might have been hacked from a stump and he was pretty strong for his size. He could take care of himself most of the time, but the truth was he was just medium-sized and Spider was a tank.

Spider reached over and slammed the piano board down. Leroy barely got his hands out of the way. A split second later and his fingers would have been busted like Popsicles.

A. J. got up and said: "That was uncalled for, Spider."

Spider turned around. A. J.'s face was familiar but he couldn't remember the name. "You zip your lip, buddy."

The room had quieted down and everyone was waiting. Pierpont was fingering his goatee himself now. He looked anxiously at A. J.

A. J. said: "Leroy here's a friend of mine."

Spider said: "Piss on him."

A. J. stepped back with a smile. "Let's you and me go do a little dancing on the gravel."

"Right now!"

They went outside to the parking lot and a lot of the people came too. Pierpont was with the two girls and they had stopped giggling. The crowd made a large circle and when Spider stepped out, he was holding a bar iron. A. J. smiled again and said wait a minute, he'd get a tire tool. The people said that was only fair. A. J. went over to his pickup and looked in the back. He was busy there for a moment, and Spider said:

"What's keeping you, buddy?"

A moment later A. J. turned around and he was holding an eight-foot fiber glass fishing rod, and at the end of the twenty-pound test line was a "Lucky 13." It was no ordinary pond bass Lucky 13 but a Muskie-size plug and it had three treble hooks. The reverse wind was on the reel and when A. J. cranked the spool and pulled the bait up, it sounded like grinding up bones. A. J. said he was ready.

Spider stepped back, and A. J. came on, flicking the rod. With the weight of that Lucky 13 bobbing on the end, it looked like he had a five-pound bass on the line.

Spider said: "Here. You can have this bar iron. You can have it, man. I don't want it." He dropped it on the ground and gave it a little push with his foot.

A. J. said: "You're sure?"

"Man, I ain't fighting you and that Lucky 13."

That ended it and everybody went back inside. Later on, Spider sat at A. J.'s table for a while and A. J. bought him a beer. But Spider did go home a little early that night.

A. J. and Leroy found Porter Seers at a supper club in Hot Springs where they served mixed drinks. Porter was in the band and was playing Leroy's sax at the time. A. J. gave the headwaiter $5 when they came in the front door, and he and Leroy walked up front like they had a table all picked out. Instead, they stepped up on the bandstand and Leroy took the sax away from Porter so fast the mouthpiece was still in his teeth. Then Leroy whipped him with his elbow and knocked him clear behind the curtain. They left through the back door before anybody could move.

Pierpont was waiting for them. "There was no trouble?" he said.

"No trouble at all," A. J. said.

They pulled out of the parking lot and were half a block down the street before they heard the sirens. Pierpont shivered and kept driving.

On the way back to Lepanto A. J. said: "Leroy, you being without a band is like a preacher without a church. It ain't right. Got any ideas?"

"Well, there's Will Durst. He's a pretty fair git-picker. Last I heard of Will he was over in West Memphis. He'd be a good lead guitar, though I don't know him personally."

"We'll find him," A. J. said and looked at Pierpont. "We're fixing to put together a band for Leroy, and it might take a while, Pierpont. You're welcome to string along and I don't mind saying we'd be glad to have you. We might could use the advice of a college man. Right, Leroy?"

"I doubt it, but it won't hurt."

"What do you say, Pierpont?"

"Well . . ."

A. J. said: "You got nothing on the fire right now with your tuna business all washed up. We'll get your car fixed later and you can go on and do as you please."

Pierpont chose his words carefully and looked down the highway. "I am pleased to be asked. Yes, I am gratified. But I must tell you the truth. It sounds slightly dangerous."

"Aw, go on, Pierpont," Leroy said.

They stopped at a liquor store on the edge of town and bought two six packs of Falstaff and a bag of ice. The beer was gone when they got to Lepanto.

They found Will Durst with Buster Leach's band at the Drummer's Club in West Memphis, and it happened to be the night that Will got fired. Will was a big, quiet boy from Calf's Neck, Arkansas, over in the Fourche River country, and he loved to yodel as much as he loved the guitar. Yodeling was a natural talent with Will and he was proud of his ability, but Buster didn't care for it and refused to work it into the show.

A. J., Leroy, and Pierpont were sitting just below the bandstand when Will put down his guitar, stepped out to the front of the platform, and started yodeling at the top of his lungs. It was beautiful and wild and loud enough to shake loose a landslide. Buster didn't like it at all and fired Will on the spot. He was kind of nasty about it.

Being fired in public didn't set with Will. He had dignity and it ran deep. He stepped outside and a few minutes later came back and went after Buster with a bicycle chain. He ran Buster clear to the Mississippi River before he lost him in a field of soybeans.

A. J. and Leroy were impressed. They got with Will later, and Leroy told him what was going on.

"That's right. I'm starting a band and I ain't got nothing against you yodelers. We'll make it a part of the show whenever we can. A little here and there won't hurt a thing. This here is A. J. Poole. They call him the Watermelon Kid. I'm Leroy Scroggins, and you won't need that bicycle chain."

Will said fine.

That night outside the Cypress Motel next to the Shell Truck Stop in West Memphis Will did a little yodeling before he turned in. He started out loud and fast but toward the end he got soft and sweet and finished up with a rendition of "The Indian Love Call" that was so melodious it would have made a gangster cry.

They got Thurmond Spooner and Lawrence "Pepper" Coe from Kirby Fernwood's band one night in Forrest City after the Pink Slipper closed and Thurmond caught Kirby in bed with Thurmond's wife, Bunny, at the Magnolia Hotel. Thurmond went a little wild. He knocked Bunny down and chased Kirby into the street. He got him around the neck and was choking him to death in a hammerlock against a fireplug when A. J. pulled him off. Kirby's eyes were bugged out and he sat there wheezing and gagging. It sounded like someone shuffling cards. Thurmond wanted to go back up-stairs and finish Bunny off, but A. J. and Leroy convinced him it wouldn't do his career any good to spend twenty years in Cummins Prison.

"She ain't worth that," Thurmond said with certainty, and joined up with the band. Pepper came along to keep him company.

Thurmond played the drums. He was as big as a door and had a jaw shaped like a spade. He came from Piggott, Arkansas, and had to go back there all of the time because of his mother, Enis, who suffered from two ailments: lumbago and Hinson's Disease, a malady that attacks the nape of the neck and is called by some Hinson's Scratch. It produces a terrible itch, and between that and her lumbago, Enis found very little time for happiness. Only when Thurmond came to see her and when he brought her fried dill pickles, did she feel like making it through the day. She said the fried pickles made her lumbago better. But there was nothing on earth that could help that Hinson's Disease, and she scratched incessantly.

Pepper was from Shell Lake, Arkansas, and he was not what you'd call handsome. He was dark and hairy and he had bad acne. Leroy used to say he had a face like a dirty ash-tray. Pepper was also skinny and had a neck so long that when he was spruced up, he looked a little like a turkey wearing a coat.

Pepper got his name because of the way he could eat hot peppers; peppers from Louisiana and Texas and Mexico, red ones, green ones, yellow ones, stringy ones and eyeball-size peppers with or without seeds. His favorites were Mamacita Bullets packed in Reynosa, Mexico. He didn't really care for the taste of peppers all that much, but ate them religiously because somebody had once told him that they would help burn out the acne. And Pepper would do anything to get rid of those pimples.

The night he had kissed Mary Nell Sharp at the FrosTop in Shell Lake, Mary Nell had gasped. She had come away from that kiss fanning herself with her purse and sucking air. And she had called Lawrence Coe names like Fireball and Dragon

Mouth and Pepper, and Pepper was the one that stuck. Mary Nell said later her lips had burned for a week.

Pepper played bass, and if he was smoking marijuana and was as high as the moon, he could thomp the people right out of their seats. He could also play rhythm guitar. Of all the boys, Pepper hated the roadhouse rat race most of all. He was always telling the others that he was going to quit one day and become a pharmacist. And he carried a book on pharmacology with him always.

They happened on Randolph "Doodle Socket" Purvis quite by accident. They were driving one day on State Highway 1 up near Jonesboro. A. J. and Pierpont were in the lead in A. J.'s pickup and Leroy and the others were trailing in Leroy's 1950 four-door Ford.

When they came by Randolph's house, he was out on the front porch. It was a dogtrot house. The radio was sitting on the steps turned all the way up. Randolph was singing and dancing up and down the breezeway, and he had his eyes closed.

A. J. saw him first and stopped the pickup so fast Pierpont almost choked to death on a mouthful of peanuts.

A. J. said: "Look at that scutter dance!"

Pierpont looked, wide-eyed and clutching his throat, and A. J. signaled the others over to the shoulder. Everybody got out and watched Randolph.

"He looks like a drunken windmill," Pierpont commented.

"I'll tell you what," A. J. said, "you won't find too many guys can move like that. Reminds me of one of them Watutsis or something. Anybody see *King Solomon's Mines?*"

Leroy said: "Don't sing too bad, either."

Pepper said: "He's kinda short. Young, too. Looks about twelve."

Randolph was short, about five feet, maybe a little shorter, but he was seventeen years old.

A. J. said: "You want to talk to him, Leroy?"

"Let's go."

They walked over to the house and Leroy did the talking. Leroy asked him where did he learn to sing and dance like that.

"Like what?"

"A Watutsi or something," Leroy said.

"You saying I dance like a nigger?"

"Aw, no. It's good. Real good."

Randolph hesitated a moment then said: "It just comes over me sometimes."

"You mean like a magic thing or can you do it all of the time?"

"What are you getting at?"

"You got good moves, son. Real good. Maybe the best I've seen. And your singing's fine. But what I want to know is can you dance like that as a regular thing?"

"Depends on how I feel."

"What if you was to get paid real good money?"

"What's real good money?"

"Ten dollars a night."

"I'd apt to feel like it permanent."

Randolph didn't even tell his mother good-bye and said his old man was over to his cousin Waldo's getting fried. He left without turning off the radio.

Randolph became the singer and eventually the frontliner with the band. He was a pretty good singer, but he was a first-class wiggler, maybe as good as Elvis Presley. That's where he got his name, not from Elvis, but from his moves. Thurmond pinned it on him when he said: "There ain't nothing wiggles like that except doodle socking fishing." That kind of fishing is a technique where the fisherman sticks his pole and bait in the water and wiggles and twists the pole and the bait to draw the fish.

Doodle liked the name, and it wasn't long before he had a high opinion of himself. He didn't think Elvis was half as good as people made him out to be. In fact, he hated him. He'd have a picture of Elvis, and he'd tack it up to the wall and throw darts at it. Or he would draw crooked, black moustaches on every picture of Elvis he could lay his hands on. And every time they went by the Silver Moon up in Newport, where Elvis had played, he'd spit out the window, even if it was raining. Things like that.

3

AFTER DOODLE SOCKET came into the group, they named the band "the Hot-Lick Lads," and Leroy sat down with A. J. and Pierpont to talk business. Leroy said they could handle the bookings and the money and take 10 percent off the top.

A. J. said thanks but no because it would be a sometime thing.

"'Sometime thing'?"

A. J. explained that he had other business and traveling to do. He added that he would be with the band off and on but not to count on it permanent and that when he was around, he would pay his own way. Then he said: "But Pierpont here has real good business sense. Besides, he's older. Nearly thirty."

"Jesus! Really?"

They looked at Pierpont.

They were sitting in Deena's Cafe in Forrest City and Pierpont rose to the occasion.

"Since I have known you, Kid, you have saved one life from drowning, my own, prevented one murder, possibly two, avoided one bad fight with commendable finesse, helped a man start a band and retrieve his saxophone. And that does not even take into consideration the things I have heard about which, by my calculation, bring the prevented murders to possibly three and the rescue of drowning victims to three—at least!"

Pierpont shook his head and looked at Leroy. "I do not know what it is, but that kind of coincidence is food for serious thought in any enduring or for that matter mutually beneficial relationship. I don't know what it is about the Kid, maybe he has a great gift. On the other hand, it may be a curse. Whatever it is, that kind of man bears watching and some looking after by one known for his prudence and perspicacity." Pierpont smiled.

"Pierpont," Leroy said, "what in the hell are you driving at?"

Pierpont sighed and sat back down. "I'm staying with the Kid."

"Well, all right then," Leroy said. "Why didn't you say so?"

A. J. looked at Pierpont and grinned.

A. J. and Pierpont drove back to DeValls that afternoon. They took a few days to get Pierpont's car back in working order then drove up to Lepanto to conclude the sale of the house. A. J. was paid $2,000 and he put it in the safe his mother had kept in her bedroom. They fooled around for another week or so, and A. J. said: "Let's go look in on Leroy and them."

A. J. had been trying to find somebody to run the boat dock and couldn't. He stopped by the restaurant and told Alvin he'd still have to do it for the time being. Alvin had been studying, and his books were spread out on the counter.

"You can't get decent help these days, hey, man?" Alvin said and grinned.

They found Leroy and the band at a joint called "The Big Time" in North Little Rock run by Charlie McCarthy. His name was really Turner Redfield, but people called him Charlie McCarthy because he had a wooden face that almost never changed expression. The band's engagement lasted only a couple of weeks and the boys were not paid the second week because Charlie was raided by a gang of police in knee boots for keeping a whorehouse in the back. Charlie's register and safe were emptied during the raid and Charlie's car was stolen. In spite of that, Charlie didn't move a muscle in his face when they carted him off to jail.

A. J. spotted the boys $100 from the sale of the house, and they headed west on Highway 70 to another engagement in Cairo, Illinois. It was late October, but it was a hot day. The temperature was up in the eighties and the boys drove with the windows down and their feet and instruments sticking out. Leroy's Ford looked like a porcupine.

They met Rainbow Wimberly in Coy's restaurant just outside of Hazen, Arkansas, when they stopped for lunch. The flies were warmed up and sounded like hamburger meat frying. "Colonial is Good Bread" was stenciled on the screen door. Coy served hamburgers and barbecue and cold drinks in scratched and sometimes greasy glasses. Rainbow was the waitress.

She had big, moist eyes, wore a tight, black uniform, and had a waist so tiny you wanted to scream. Her legs were perfect, as smooth as bamboo, her hair was honey-blonde and curled at the shoulders, and her chest danced when she walked.

Rainbow didn't like being a waitress and she didn't like Coy, who smelled like grease and Juicy Fruit gum, which he chewed a pack at a time. She had been looking out of the window at Leroy's car and considering. The paint was flaky, the tires were as slick as cannonballs, and the muffler had roared when they drove in. But she could see the instruments in the back. Rainbow said:

"You guys with a band?"

"Meet the Hot-Lick Lads," Leroy said.

"Pleased to," Rainbow said. "I envy that. One of these days I'm gonna get on a bus out there on that big, fast Highway 70 and ride right into Little Rock in style. You wait and see."

Leroy told her they were on their way to Cairo, Illinois, but that first they had to stop in Piggott to see Thurmond's mother, and that she was welcome to come along.

"There is no future in hamburgers," Leroy said and everyone agreed.

Rainbow did things in a hurry. She nodded and went back to change out of her uniform. When she came out front again, Coy was following. He was mad, and the veins in his neck stood out like pods on purple hull peas. He was banging things around and kicking the cabinets, and he told her she wasn't going anywhere.

The boys all stood up behind their stools prepared to defend the lady's rights. A. J. hadn't said anything and he could feel Pierpont place a warning hand on his shoulder. Coy was a pretty big guy.

Coy said: "You get back there in your uniform!"

Rainbow came around the counter and told Leroy not to bother with a tip, and then she looked at Coy.

"Why don't you go take a flying fuck at the moon?"

Coy followed her to the door, but she slammed it in his face, and he didn't come outside.

After that, they drove on to Piggott. Rainbow rode up front between Leroy and Doodle Socket. She had a copy of *Screen Stars* magazine and read it from cover to cover.

"I wouldn't have no trouble being a movie star," she said.

"You got my vote," Leroy told her.

Doodle Socket sneered but didn't say anything.

On the way up to Piggott, Leroy's car broke down in a small town south of Jonesboro. The trouble was a broken water hose, and when they pulled steaming and hissing into a gas station, Rainbow, who was wearing a skirt and sweater, got out and crossed the street to the drugstore to get a Coke. That's all she did, just cross the street, but it took her two minutes.

Rainbow had the best slow walk there ever was. There wasn't much traffic through town that day, but all of it, walking or riding, stopped. She ambled this way and that, turned and looked around with her head raised, and then she inhaled and held it, letting out a little air at a time and inhaling again to keep her chest full. The straw hat league was out on the bench next to the drugstore, and they could barely stand it. They all looked hard and hungrily, and their toes curled in their shoes. But when Rainbow walked past and said, "Hi, fellas," their eyes dropped like shades coming down and they studied the sidewalk with great intensity. When at last she entered the drugstore, a few of the older boys took off their straw hats and began fanning themselves furiously.

Nobody was going to move from that bench. No, sir. The wife of one of the men had been watching from across the street and decided it was time she had a talk with her husband. She waited until Rainbow was in the drugstore and then came over, taking little quick steps, like she was stepping on a trail of ants. But the man said to her before she could utter a word: "You go on home woman." And his eyes were flashing with magnificent guilt.

Then and there A. J. and Leroy realized what an asset Rainbow could be. They all had a conference while she was in the drugstore and everybody but Doodle Socket agreed they ought to find something for Rainbow to do in the band.

Doodle Socket said: "Bet she can't sing a note, and she don't know the first thing about a guitar. I asked her."

"Well, let's see," A. J. said.

After they got Leroy's car fixed, they drove down a dirt road to a place that was private and quiet. Rainbow looked slightly worried and asked A. J. what the hell was this. A. J. said to take it easy. She was going to have an audition.

"Hey, really?" Rainbow was pleased.

The boys took out their instruments and gave her an audition. It was over in less than a minute, and everybody knew Rainbow couldn't sing a note. Rainbow said, "I can't sing. Sorry about that."

"I told you so," Doodle Socket said.

Rainbow straightened up and glared at Doodle Socket, and A. J. said: "That's it. Hold that, Rainbow, and walk around the car. Take your time, honey. Just like back in town."

From then on, the band was known as "the Highway 70 Six," and they worked Rainbow into the show with a spotlight and standing routine. All they did was train the spot on her table and introduce her as Miss Rainbow Wimberly of Hazen, Arkansas. Rainbow would get up, smile, smooth down her dress over her thighs, and then turn around real slow. Sometimes she would walk around the table. That's all there was to it, but there wouldn't be a dry lip on any man or boy in the place. She was probably the best stander in the business, and she was a hit every time.

Rainbow even looked good when she was spitting mad, and she took very little sass. She knew how to fight with her fists and her teeth and with her high-heeled shoe if things really got serious. One thing, though, about Rainbow. She had a loose eye. It didn't bother her very often, just when she was extra mad or terribly excited. Then, she couldn't control it. Her left eye was normal and steady, but the other one rolled. It was pretty unnerving to a stranger and the boys never really got used to it either.

Rainbow became Leroy's girl, but it was not a faithful or a flawless thing. Eventually, they became man and wife under that Common Law and they had a couple of kids. She settled on Leroy because he was the leader of the band and he was around more, but she was crazy about A. J., too. The trouble was that A. J. and Leroy had made a deal. It happened that day when Rainbow was in the drugstore and they had flipped a coin. They flipped a 1944 quarter in the gas station that hit the pavement of the apron, rolled into the garage and under a creeper and down into the drive-over pit before it finally came to rest with the spread wings of the eagle face up. Leroy had called tails.

"Well, that's that," A. J. said, and he began avoiding Rainbow.

They got to Piggott late in the afternoon and went with Thurmond to see his mother. Enis was in a bad way. Thurmond had picked up some fried dill pickle sandwiches in Jonesboro, and they made her feel a little better, but she was having a terrible time on account of the Hinson's Scratch. She couldn't keep still and was as busy as a fiddler trying to keep a scratch ahead of that itch. It was so bad that Pepper and Doodle started doing it too. They were sitting in Enis' front room and pretty soon it began to sound like a puppy at a screen door.

When Enis noticed Pepper and Doodle, her eyes got full of tears. "They done gone and catched it, too," she cried. "I ain't good for nothing in this world! And oh, Lord, how I hate this awful itch!" And then she ran from the room, bawling like a child.

They spent the night in a motel and everybody took a shower. Doodle and Pepper were all right in the morning.

Before they left for Cairo, Rainbow came by A. J.'s room and said: "I like you, Kid. How come you don't like me?"

"That ain't it," A. J. said, and he told her about the coin.

Rainbow's right eye began to roll slightly. "Flipped a coin?"

she screamed. "What the hell do you think I am? The last can of beer or something?"

After that Rainbow felt that she was bound by no code and slept where she pleased. Even with Doodle Socket. But not with A. J., except for once on a very special occasion when the rules were suspended. Leroy knew what was going on, but he understood those things. Leroy said Rainbow wandered like a marble in a bathtub.

Cairo, Illinois. That's where the Ohio and the Mississippi rivers come together from east and west bringing the snows and rains from the whole country and it's not a good place to be in a lengthy downpour. The bridges are arched like a cat's back and they are higher than any building in Louisiana. A lot of water goes through there.

You don't say Cairo like you pronounce Cairo in Egypt, but like in Karo nut pie or Karo Syrup. It's not much of a place these days; you wouldn't want to stop there except maybe for gas, but it used to be a pretty fair town, with a couple of nice hotels and two or three roadhouses where you could have some fun. One of them was Chester Bingo's Blue Swan north of town on U.S. Highway 51.

The Blue Swan was a two-story roadhouse, and it was painted black with orange doors and windows like Halloween. The swan hung from a light pole out front and its eyes were red blinking lights and the body was light blue like a Bunsen Burner flame. Chester did a good business. He had two bands, a paved parking lot, and the lot even had two big floodlights and a bouncer who watched the cars. There were four bouncers inside, two on each floor. The gambling was upstairs.

The Highway 70 Six played an extended engagement of two, then six, then four more weeks and the last four they were the headlined band. The people loved them. Rainbow astounded them in the spotlight. Doodle drove them crazy with his moves, and they even liked Will's yodeling. The money was good. The boys built up their reserves and Doodle Socket bought himself a car, a black '53 T-Bird with yellow streaks of jagged lightning painted on the sides which A. J. said reminded him of Captain Marvel.

The boys might have stayed longer at the Blue Swan if it hadn't been for the shooting. It happened right after the first of the year when a farm boy from Padukah got tired of watching the pit boss, Breedlove Pitcock, taking away the money in the strongbox under the dealer's hole at the crap table. The boy pulled a .25 automatic from his boot and shot one of Breedlove's ears off. They closed the place for a couple of weeks after that.

The boys spent part of that winter playing spots over in Cape Girardeau and Poplar Bluff, Missouri, and for a while at a joint down in Blytheville, Arkansas. They traveled around like a caravan with Doodle Socket leading the way in his streaked T-Bird. Doodle rode alone most of the time. He drove fast and loved to leave rubber, at zero or seventy miles an hour. His T-Bird came with superchargers and Doodle's car sounded like an F-86 on afterburner. If you weren't ready for it, it would snap your head off. He loved that car as much as he hated Elvis, and he wouldn't let you eat or drink or smoke for fear something would happen to his upholstery, which was imitation leopard. He had a pair of baby shoes dangling from the mirror, Confederate flags on both rear aerials and mudguards with ruby-red, heart-shaped reflectors. He had a regular horn, an air horn, and a Bermuda bell with the pedal on the floor. When Doodle came to town with everything going, the colored people were appalled and the white people jumped like rabbits.

Doodle and Rainbow had a little thing going there for a while after he got his car. She liked tooling around in that flashy T-Bird and maybe as a reward or maybe it was out of kindness, Rainbow taught him about sex. They would be driving along, sometimes right in town, and Rainbow would disappear below the seat so the other boys couldn't see her, and Doodle Socket would start ringing that Bermuda bell like the world was on fire. At other times, they would just disappear together. The boys found them one day that winter tucked away in a deserted campground near Portageville, Missouri. They sneaked up on them but couldn't see inside because the windows were all steamed up.

Early that spring, two things happened: Doodle almost got himself killed and the boys learned that Rainbow was pregnant. Doodle's accident happened at the Blue Swan, which was open again.

"You're a pain in the ass," Leroy said to Doodle Socket. It was the second time he had said it in two days.

Doodle Socket grinned. "They say that about all the stars." He was wearing a pink turtleneck sweater and tight black pants and was smoking a filter-tip Kings that was as long as a pencil. He still coughed some, but he was about to master it. He also had grown sideburns down to his jaws that were shaped like porkchops, and he had just bought his first pair of elevator shoes.

When the band reopened at the Blue Swan, Chester had given Doodle star billing and the sign out front said:

The Highway 70 Six
with
The Sensational
DOODLE SOCKET

Chester liked him. "That boy can outsway a willow in a high wind. Anything he wants, let him have it." Chester gave him more free beer than anybody else and every once in a while he'd tell Breedlove to let him win at blackjack.

"Like last night," Leroy said.

The night before Doodle Socket had got so high on three joints that he had tried to fly off the bandstand. They were playing "The Love Sick Blues," and Doodle was doing everything he could to put Elvis in the shade. The sweat was flying off his forehead and he was screaming like a hurricane. He was still singing when he climbed up on Leroy's piano and took to the air.

He landed on a table and fell down among an instant midden of beer bottles, glasses, French fried potatoes, steak bones, knives, forks, and A-1 and catsup with his head wedged between the struts of a chair and his shoulders pinned under part of a table and a toppled woman and with the curved fragment of a broken pitcher pressed against his throat like a scimitar. If anyone had moved the wrong way, it would have slit his throat like a Vienna sausage.

Doodle had lain there trying not to breathe, and luckily nobody moved the wrong way. But it took the bouncers a couple of minutes to set him free.

"The other guys don't like it," Leroy said.

"Don't like what?"

"The way you been stepping out on your own. Doing what you damn please up there and not staying with the rest of us."

"That's your problem."

"You got the big head, Doodle Socket. Watch it."

Leroy spoke to A. J. about it and that night just before one of Doodle Socket's numbers, Leroy stepped up to the mike with A. J. and they went into a routine. Leroy played the star and A. J. the psychiatrist.

"Well, son," A. J. said, "so you got a problem. What's the matter?"

Leroy said: "I cain't sing."

"Go on."

"I cain't pick a guitar."

"I see."

"I cain't act or sing neither."

"Well, what else is wrong?"

"I'm the star."

Doodle Socket was surprised and not pleased. He didn't care for ridicule and announced to the audience that he would not sing any more that night and started to step down off the bandstand. Doodle Socket didn't weigh 125 pounds with his pockets full of nickles, and Bubba Smart, who was sitting in the front row with his girl, Laverne, took hold of him in midair and sat him down hard on the table like a wooden dummy. Doodle's legs flopped up and his eyes blinked.

Bubba said: "You ain't going nowhere, shorty. Me and Laverne come to hear you sing."

Bubba was a big guy with a flat head and a crew cut. His

hands were like hooks and he had no hips. He was wearing a T-shirt and his Camels were rolled in his sleeve.

Doodle Socket said: "Don't you ever call me shorty!" He came up from the table onto Bubba's neck, going for his eyes. Bubba staggered back about two steps, picked Doodle off, held him up for a last look and pitched him over five tables. Doodle slid off the last table in between the scattering of people and right through a thin pasteboard wall and into the darkness on the other side.

The other members of the band stood up, and the music stopped. Leroy went to look for Doodle Socket, and A. J. stepped in front of Bubba.

"Good evening," A. J. said. He moved his feet forward and pinned Bubba's toes to the floor. Then he gave Bubba a fast shove. Bubba's eyes opened wide with surprise and he went down like tall timber.

The bouncers were moving over, but it was too late. Laverne kicked the table into A. J.'s stomach, and when he doubled over, she narrowly missed his head with a full bottle of Schlitz. The glass and the beer went flying, and a woman who got wet jumped on Laverne and they hit the floor clawing and biting. Bubba got up and came after A. J. Some of Bubba's friends moved in to help and that brought the boys off the bandstand. The bouncers couldn't stop it now.

Leroy found Doodle Socket on the other side of the wall and held his head in his lap like a baby. Leroy slapped his face and rubbed his cheeks and called his name, but Doodle was out cold.

It was a terrible fight. Tables were splintering, chairs whizzed through the air, and people were bleeding and crying. Pierpont was hiding behind the piano, shielding his eyes and head from flying glass and wood. One of Bubba's friends found him and jerked him up. "You're with this goddam band, ain't you, buddy?"

"I haven't the faintest idea what you're . . ."

But the man hit him anyway and Pierpont fell among the ruins.

People were trying to get out the door, but tables and

knocked-out men and screaming women were in the way, and the people fought each other to escape. Some of them broke a window and crawled through, bleeding and running for their cars. It was a mess.

A. J. was having a lot of trouble with Bubba, who had him down with his neck pinned under the bottom of a chair. A. J. couldn't fight back because the legs of the chair got in his way. Bubba kept hitting him in the stomach and yelling "You son of a bitch! You son of a bitch!" every time his fist came down.

Rainbow tried to help him once, but Laverne headed her off and they fell to the floor with Rainbow's beautiful legs kicking wildly in the air. Chester waded through the mob with a blackjack, knocking out the winners of individual fights and letting the survivors go. He took a swing at Bubba and missed and Bubba grabbed him by the belt and heaved him over a table. Chester got up somewhat dazed and he still had his blackjack, but he didn't take any more swings at Bubba.

A. J. was in a bad way, and it might have been really serious if it hadn't been for Will, who finally got close enough to Bubba to put him out with a piano leg. But he had to hit him twice and the second time the roller came off in his hands. "Jesus!" Will said and rubbed his hands because they were stinging. Then he and Thurmond and Pepper took Bubba by the feet and shoulders and carried him outside where they seined him in a borrow ditch. The cops were on the way by then.

When it was all over, A. J. found Leroy and Doodle Socket in the storeroom, which was what lay on the other side of the partition. Doodle Socket had come to, and Leroy was looking into his eyes like a brain surgeon.

A. J. said: "How's the matinee idol?"

"He'll live. Say, you look bad yourself."

"Feel it."

"What hit you?"

"Bubba Smart."

"How're the others?"

Will poked his head in through the partition and announced: "Everybody's fine." Rainbow, Pepper, and Thurmond were behind him. Pierpont looked in after a moment and his goatee was bloody.

Leroy said: "Doodle Socket, I was fixing to chew your ass but good, and you know why, but I'll let it go. How's the head?"

Doodle Socket said: "Being thrown through a wall ain't no picnic." The others all agreed with him. "But I guess I'm all right. Wonder if Elvis ever got hisself throwed through a wall?"

Leroy said he didn't know. That he didn't think so.

Doodle Socket grinned. "Naw," he said. "Reckon old Elvis couldn't take a thing like that."

4

IT WAS A Sunday night. The Blue Swan was closed and A. J. was sitting out in front of the RiverVue Motel watching the sun go down. Leroy and Rainbow were in their room. Doodle Socket was out driving his car. Pepper was studying his book on pharmacology. Thurmond was on the phone to his mother, and Will was down by the river, out of sight below some trees, yodeling at the sunset. Pierpont was in the motel room working on a blackjack.

Pretty soon he came outside and sat down in an aluminum chair next to A. J. He looked determined and very serious. A. J. sneaked a glance at him out of the corner of his eye and waited. Pierpont stroked his goatee, which he had twisted to a point as sharp as a hat pin. He rested his hands on the arms of his chair like a gunfighter and narrowed his eyes.

The seconds ticked by and then Pierpont yelled and whipped out the blackjack and brought it down hard against the arm of the chair. "Whop!" he yelled again with pleasure. "Whop. Whop. Whop. That ought to fix any son of a bitch who lays a hand on you or me!" The arm of the chair was crushed like a beer can.

"Let me see that thing," A. J. said. He looked it over. Pierpont had made it himself out of a piece of pipe filled with lead and wrapped in boot leather. It had a braided handle and a loop on the end. A. J. handed it back to Pierpont. "You don't need that. A blackjack can get you into serious trouble."

"On the contrary. I do need it. Henceforth I will not be without it. I am not a strong man and I need an equalizer. This!" He slapped the other arm of the chair.

"You're gonna ruin that chair if you keep that up."

Pierpont examined the damaged chair, and he was satisfied. Then he slipped the blackjack into his pocket and patted his hip.

"Let me tell you about blackjacks," A. J. said. "You get in a brawl and you're only using your fists and you're OK. But you pull a blackjack or knucks or a knife and that changes the rules. Then you're liable to find yourself going up against something you can't handle."

Pierpont said: "No. I've seen enough to know. They use everything in a fight. Bottles, cracked or whole, clubs, glasses, sticks, chairs, legs off of tables, crowbars, and antlers. No, sir. A blackjack is a good thing."

"Well, have it your way."

"I will." And he got up and went back into his room.

Leroy came down the walk and pulled up Pierpont's mangled chair. He looked questioningly at A. J.

"Pierpont's been trying out his blackjack."

"Oh."

Leroy sat down. He looked worried.

"She's pregnant, Kid."

It was quiet for a moment while A. J. thought that over.

"Well, don't look at me," A. J. said.

"I wasn't. I'm the father all right. She says I am."

"You are."

"I guess it's about time she made a trip back to Hazen. Funny, I'd noticed she'd blimped a little, but I figured it was them fries and Cokes she eats all the time. It's a wonder her face don't look like Pepper's."

Leroy wanted to talk so A. J. let him.

"She says she sneaked off to the doctor last week and he says there's no doubt about it. Baby's due in June."

"That soon?"

"Just around the corner."

"You mention Hazen to her?" Leroy nodded. "What'd she say?"

"Slapped me with *Screen Stars*."

"Well, looks like she'd want to be with her folks to have her baby."

"She ain't mad about that."

39

"What then?"

"I ain't going with her."

"I see. So she hit you with the magazine?" Leroy nodded again, and A. J. said: "At least Rainbow lets you know how she feels."

"Uh huh. I can't take the time away from the band. And hell, Kid, she's liable to swarm anywhere. That baby could be born in a back seat or in a bar ditch. Hell, even in a swamp. I don't want that."

"No. That wouldn't be right."

"I got her a bus ticket for tomorrow morning."

The bus left at 9:30, and Rainbow wasn't a bit happy about a two-hundred-mile ride to Hazen. She moved kind of slow and painfully and her face was a little broken out from the fries and a craving she'd had lately for banana splits. The boys were all worried about her. They kissed her good-bye and said what a fine-looking bus that Greyhound was and how much they wished they could take a trip somewhere.

Rainbow kept her eyes on Leroy the whole time and all she said was, "Yeah."

Finally, Leroy stepped up and kissed her good-bye, leaning forward like at a fountain, and then he punched her lightly on the arm and said: "Take it easy, kid. Keep in touch."

Rainbow got on the bus crying and sneering at the same time. The bus driver, a thin, older man with a hooked chin and pious, smoldering eyes, gave Leroy a dirty look and slammed the door so hard a woman sitting up front reading the St. Louis *Post-Dispatch* let out a startled scream.

The bus pulled out, and the boys waved good-bye. Rainbow waved back, but she didn't even look at Leroy.

On the way back to the motel, Leroy said to A. J. confidentially: "You know this is our first kid. And there might be more where this one come from. The way I see it, I don't want to start a precedent. If I was to go back with her now, she'd expect it the next time and after that too. Once is a gift. Twice is a habit."

"You ain't made the gift yet," A. J. pointed out.

"Well, anyway, I don't think women really expect it when

they have kids. It's woman's business, and a man has no place."

"You sure about that?"

"Naw. I'm just talking."

After Cairo, the boys played another brief engagement over in Cape Girardeau and then took a little time off. Leroy hadn't heard anything from Rainbow, so after about a week he called her. He got Rainbow's mother, Aranell, first. Aranell put down the phone hard and yelled for Rainbow:

"IT'S on the phone!"

Rainbow sounded in high spirits, maybe too high. She said she was doing fine, didn't miss anybody and that she was going to name the baby Lester if it was a boy after one of her old boyfriends.

There was a pause on the line.

"Did you hear me, Leroy?"

"Yeah, I did."

"Maybe I just ought to call it 'Polecat' after you know who!"

"Aw, go on, Rainbow."

The boys left the Cape on a Sunday afternoon and headed south. Their next date was down at Flossie's and after that at Molly Fitlowe's place in Marked Tree, but that was two weeks off. Doodle Socket left them in Portageville, Missouri. He said he wanted to go to Memphis to see an agent named Trent Dangerfield about Hollywood and New York and that he'd meet them at Flossie's if he hadn't been asked to go on the Ed Sullivan Show.

After Doodle headed for Memphis, the boys turned west toward the mountains. It was a good time for traveling. Late April. The trees all had fresh tops and the birds seemed to fly higher and faster. A chill left over from winter still lay in the valleys in the morning and night, but the long parts of the day were warm and sunny. The boys were in no hurry. Leroy put Rainbow and Hazen in the back of his mind the way you put a bill in a drawer for payment at another time. They took two days to reach Thayer, Missouri. There, they stopped and loaded up with beer and whiskey and then drove south and west.

The boys didn't have a care in the world. They were off for a place called "Nowhere in Particular," taking their own sweet time. It was good just to get away from the roadhouse rat race—the noise and the smoke and the fights. And the mountains did something for the boys. Their devilment went away and hid. They were always hard up for money and watched a dollar like a hawk watches a hen, but now they didn't care. There were no girls, but they could talk of them and magnify the soft pleasures and lie and drool and never have to be bothered with a single woman.

They drank and smoked around their campfires and when the drunken evenings deepened and the fire burned low and the stars came down close and were as blue as Christmas lights, the boys dreamed of many things that could never be.

Sometimes, they played music down by a river in the late afternoons and evenings. They played only for themselves without an audience and the winds carried it away. And it was a different kind of music, the kind no roadhouse would allow. It was the sound of "O Susannah" and "Across the Wide Missouri" and an almost forgotten "Carolina Rose."

Those were fine nights and they were especially good for Will and yodeling. You might see him out there alone on a sandbar or tucked away in a hollow with his head raised like a hungry bird, and he made a beautiful sound. The boys loved it, and Pierpont would listen with his eyes closed. A. J. used to say he wished he could yodel like that and Leroy would say "It sounds all right, don't it?" And when it was very late and the fire was almost out and the water seemed to run the quietest of all, the boys fell into a deep and glorious sleep and slept in the shade till noon.

But it didn't last.

A couple of weeks later, when they came down again into the flat valley, that easygoing, careless spirit that had stopped time in the mountains left them. They grew restless and alert. The interlude was over, and the soft sounds of the wind and water gave way to the racket of horns and the whine of trucks. It was time again to hurry.

A. J. and Leroy were driving fast and close, and they laid on their horns. The boys cracked beer after beer. They drank fast and their chins were foamy. They leaned out of the windows and yelled and made faces at farm girls who yelled and made faces back. An earsplitting sound from Leroy's rotten muffler rattled the windows of stores in towns when they passed through. And the grain elevators swept by and the wide open fields. And the tracks were hooting with trains.

They pulled into a gas station near Des Arc, and they were all panting as if they had been in a footrace. A. J. climbed down from behind the wheel. "Here, you take the pickup," he told Pierpont. "Thurm, you keep the old man company. I'm gonna ride with the beer for a while." He slipped in the front seat beside Leroy and reached back and opened a can of Falstaff.

The owner of the station wasn't there, but a Negro who was about forty slid off an oil drum and came over chewing on a stick of straw. He kind of hunch-rolled his shoulders when he walked and he had a grin on his face as big as a banana for no reason at all. Leroy told him to fill the tank, and the Negro said:

"Sure, man."

A. J. looked over at Leroy, his face as benign as a Buddha's, but his eyes were slit and glittering. He said plenty loud enough for the Negro to hear:

"You think we ought to let her out of the trunk?"

Leroy thought for a second with a big knot in his cheek and then he looked straight ahead. "You mean Norma Stell? Naw."

Will and Pepper in the back seat both said at the same time: "Not yet, Kid. It ain't time to let her out yet."

The Negro was just taking the nozzle from the slot. He did so real quiet and stood for a moment looking out over a bean field. His shoulders had stopped hunch rolling and his eyes had grown large and white. He came around behind the car slowly, eased off the cap and put in the nozzle, and he was looking hard at the trunk. He left the nozzle in and came around to the front and started wiping the windshield. He looked at Leroy, and when Leroy locked eyes with him, he

43

glanced away and started whistling.

The Negro said: "Been kind of hot."

Leroy nodded. "Yeah."

A. J. leaned around to the others and they had a whispered conference. Then A. J. said: "I don't know. Maybe we ought to let her out. It's kind of airtight in there. And, it *is* hot."

The others shook their heads and Leroy said: "She's all right. She ain't hurting."

The Negro finished Leroy's side and moved over to A. J.'s. He kept looking around for guns and knives and then he went back to check the nozzle. It was still running, and he knelt down quickly and tapped the trunk with two quick thumps, not too loud. There was no sound. He came back to the front and he was about half grinning and half trembling and he said to A. J.:

"You mean you got a girl in that trunk?"

"That's right."

"Well, excuse me, but I tapped back there and didn't hear nothing."

Will said: "She ain't supposed to make any noise."

The Negro looked at A. J., studying him. "I don't know, man. Like you say, it's kind of airtight in there."

A. J. shrugged.

Will said: "We aired her out up in Batesville a couple of hours back. She ain't hurting."

Pepper said: "Norma Stell can take it."

The Negro rocked back and forth on his heels and stretched a little to take a look at the whole car, and then his eyes swung to Leroy. "I ain't one to mess, but ain't that a little hard on her?"

Leroy said: "You know Norma Stell?"

"Don't believe so."

"If you did, you'd understand."

"How's that?"

Leroy shook his head. "Man, she is so ugly we got to keep her out of sight till after dark."

"Sure nuff?"

"Aw, yeah. That's right. She's rank. Don't you go open that trunk."

"Oh, I ain't. I ain't fixing to," he said and went to get the nozzle, tiptoeing to show he had every intention of leaving things exactly as they were.

Leroy paid for the gas and they told the Negro good-bye and not to worry about Norma Stell. She'd be all right. And then they drove on down to DeValls.

The boys stayed a few days with A. J. and then went up to Lepanto for their engagement at Flossie's. Pierpont was relieved to see them go and drank a pint of Jack Daniels Black Label all by himself to celebrate.

5

ONE AFTERNOON late in May, Warren Simmons and Odell Dunnaway from Gillett came by A. J.'s boat dock looking for ice, and they had forty pounds of rainbow trout in their cold box. A. J. looked at the fish and he was impressed.

"Where'd they come from?"

"Spring River up north of Hardy," Odell told him. "There's so many fish up there now they're leaning on one another."

"Go, and you'll see," Warren said.

A. J. and Pierpont were on their way the next morning, and Pierpont was still grumbling. "It's time you quit this fooling around and tended to your business. You are a man with considerable responsibilities. Now, don't look at me like that. I am serious. With your resources and my financial skills, you could be a wealthy man."

A. J. grinned. "Pierpont, you're a good old boy, but you sure do worry a lot."

On the way they stopped in Batesville to see A. J.'s aunt and uncle, Doris and Joe Lynly. Doris was his aunt on his mother's side. Joe was a retired railroad conductor who suffered occasionally from "spells."

"This won't take a minute," A. J. said as they went up the front steps.

Doris let them in with a finger to her lips.

"Shhhh," she whispered. "Joe's up in the tower. The 210 from Kansas City had a hot box up near Cotter. Two oil cars are derailed and a boxcar is wrecked on the double track. The 212 is headed the other way at full speed, but there's no way to get through to Cotter. The lines are down because of the ice storm."

Pierpont looked out of the window. The trees were green

46

and full, their shadows stretched across the street and the yards, and the windows glistened in the warm sunlight.

"Having one of his spells again?" A. J. said.

Doris nodded. "We must be very quiet. He's terribly worried and doesn't want to be disturbed." She looked uncertainly at Pierpont.

"Meet Pierpont Higgins," A. J. said. "A friend of mine. He's from Ohio."

"Really?"

"How do you do?" Pierpont said and glanced discreetly upward to the second floor.

"How long's he been up there this time?" A. J. said.

"Since yesterday. You know he calls the attic his tower. He has it all nicely arranged." She looked at Pierpont to explain. "We're on a hill here and from up there he can see for miles. He watches the trains every day when they come up the valley and stop in town." She paused a moment and said: "He's not well, you see. Ever since the accident."

"Want us to stay a while? You might need some help," A. J. said.

Pierpont shot A. J. a warning look. He was thinking there was a maniac in the attic.

They heard a door open and close in the upper part of the house and then heavy footsteps on the stairs.

"Oh, my!" Doris said.

Joe appeared on the landing. He was a tall man with deep set, dark eyes and heavy eyebrows. He had not shaved. He was wearing a heavy black coat over his conductor's uniform and the collar flaps were up around his ears. His conductor's hat was pressed tightly on his head and he was wearing mittens.

He stopped at the foot of the stairs and eyed them sternly.

"I was about to go myself, but I see you've come. What have you got to report? Well, don't just stand there. I'm needed back in the tower."

"They flagged the 212, Joe," A. J. said. "Everything's OK. We just talked to Cotter."

"That's funny. I couldn't get through."

47

"You can now. The lines are fixed."

"It's about time. That's no way to run a railroad." He squinted at A. J. "It's good to see you again." Then he frowned at Pierpont. "You must be Wilson from the Little Rock office. I want a full report on this. Is that clear?"

Pierpont nodded.

"Good." Joe turned and looked for a moment out of the window. "Damn this weather!" he said and raced back up the stairs.

Doris sighed and sank into a chair. She smiled at A. J. "He'll be all right now. But I'm glad you came when you did. I don't want him to go out when he's like this."

"What set him off this time?"

"It started a couple of days ago I guess. There was a train wreck out in Oklahoma. Not a very bad one, but he read about it in the papers and he got terribly upset. I wish they didn't have to put train wrecks in the papers."

"Yeah," A. J. said and patted her shoulder. "We'll see you, Doris. Take it easy."

A. J. told Pierpont about Joe on the way to Hardy. Joe had worked for the Santa Fe and the Texas and Pacific and he was with the Missouri Pacific in Kansas City that day when he had got bumped by a switch engine and hit his head. They had retired him after that.

They got to Hardy about one and drove across the state line to pick up some beer and ice. They came back into Arkansas and turned right at Mammoth Spring to get to the river.

They followed dirt roads through a forest of oak and cedar and came down in a deep hole to the river where the sycamores and willows grew. There was a long shoals there, below a horse-shoe-shaped falls. A. J. pulled up to the water and parked under a sycamore.

They saw no one else fishing, but an old bus was parked back in a hollow up a short road that ended at the base of the mountain. A high mane of grass was growing in the center of the road and thick branches of trees hung low over the top of the bus.

Pierpont laid a blanket on the bank and stretched out to

listen to the water and sleep. It was a nice day for it, and he got himself into a sleepy mood with a couple of cans of Falstaff.

A. J. waded out and fished the shoals, but landed only one trout. It was small and only jumped once. He fished another twenty minutes without another strike. He told himself he wasn't catching fish because he was thinking about that bus. It was an old bus, a GMC of about 1940 or '41. But the strange thing about it was that it was camouflaged, with green and yellow swirls that made it a little hard to see back in that hollow. The paint was fresh, too, not faded like it had been left over from the war. A. J. was curious about that.

A trout struck his bait, jumped once and spit the hook. A. J. didn't throw out again. He came back to shore, put down his rod, told Pierpont to have a nice nap and headed for the bus.

And he didn't pay any attention when Pierpont said: "I would not fool with that bus if I were you."

A. J. approached the bus whistling and trying to smile. There was music coming from a radio. Elvis Presley singing "Blue Suede Shoes." After Elvis, the announcer came on talking fast about the speedway races that night up in Koshkonong, Missouri, and then a singer named Bobby Pickett gave out with "The Love Sick Blues."

The lettering on the scroll in the signbox over the driver's seat said:

CHRIST OR DEATH
Rev. J. C. Wright, Esq.

What A. J. didn't but might have been interested to know was that J. C. Wright was an itinerant preacher-pilgrim who sold soap and sometimes corn whiskey and traveled under the aliases of Edgar Coldwater, Darrell MacDade, and currently, J. C. Wright, mainly because he was wanted in several midwestern states for stealing groceries and violating the Green River Ordinance against peddling. His real name was John Robert Slart. He was from Sallisaw, Oklahoma.

The shades were all down in the windows of the bus, and

as he got closer someone turned the volume on the radio up. It occurred to A. J. to lift one of the shades and take a look, but he remembered what had happened to Grady MacNeil in DeValls when Grady had done such a thing to look in on Betty Thorp. Betty had not appreciated the attention and had stroked him with a piece of stove wood.

So A. J. called out: "Hey, in there. Anybody home? Can you hear me?"

No answer, and the music was still loud.

He called again and then a third time before the music was finally turned down. The only other sound was the soft tapping of the shades against the windowsills.

Then, so quickly it made A. J. jump back, one of the shades popped up. It rolled a couple of mosquitoes flat, wrapped the pullcord around like a tassel on a diploma and revealed Miss Ivoe Slart.

She stood there with the knuckle of her little finger in her mouth, and from the waist up she was as naked as a pearl. Her breasts stood straight out like two, great red-tipped thorns, and her stomach was so flat and narrow A. J. let out a little cry. But Ivoe didn't look all that smart, sucking her knuckle, and her eyes were open just a bit too wide, giving the impression it might be kind of drafty inside.

Ivoe made the first move. As if she were savoring a lollipop, she drew her knuckle out of her mouth slowly and started to back up. Her breasts hopped a little when she stepped. A. J. looked inside the window. It was pretty cluttered in there. Magazines and papers were scattered around and there were some bottles and jars on the floor. In the back of the bus was a bed, unmade, and in the front behind the driver's seat was a stove and an icebox and a stack of boxes labeled "Vivid." Vivid was a kind of soap, and the bus smelled soapy. On the far side of the bus was a cot. There were some faded pillows on the cot.

Then A. J. saw the chain. It was a light chain, the kind you would use for a dog but strong enough so that it would take a hatchet or chisel to cut it. And it was attached to Miss Slart, to something just below her waist and under the pair of sleek, skin-tight black pants of shiny velvet she had on. She wore no shoes.

The chain stretched all the way to the front of the bus where it was padlocked to the leg of the stove, which was bolted to the floor. A. J. crawled into the bus. He picked up the chain and gave it a tug to make sure it was fastened to Ivoe. From the way she moved, he could tell it was.

"How come?" he said.

Ivoe smiled, a loose sort of smile where her lower lip sagged a little like an open drawer. She said nothing but started to move slowly down the bus toward him.

A. J. said: "How come this chain? Who does that?"

"Daddy." She kept moving and the music kept playing.

A. J. frowned. "Your daddy, huh?"

He looked again at the padlock on the stove leg and back to her. She had come very close to him now. Her shoulders were thrown back and her hands were flat against her sides. She walked right into him and said:

"You wanna danth?"

A. J. cocked his head. "How's that?"

"You wanna danth?"

A. J. slipped his arms around her tiny waist and grinned: "Let's," he said.

They hardly moved their feet. Just their bodies swayed, and A. J. squeezed great handfulls of her back. His hands crept lower and when he touched the elastic in her pants, he felt something firm and hard. He ran his fingers over it and then tapped it with his knuckle. It was something metal.

A. J. stood back and looked at Ivoe seriously.

"What the hell have you got on down there?"

Ivoe said: "It's a chasthidy belt."

A. J. stopped dancing. "A chastity belt. Christ on a crutch, girl, people don't wear them things any more!"

"Uh huh!" Ivoe said.

A. J. bent down. "Excuse me a minute. If you don't mind, I'd like to take a look at this."

What struck him right off was how polished and shiny it was. Someone had taken some time to do that. It had been cut from a strip of sheet metal and the edges had been curled up and flattened so it wouldn't scratch or cut. It was hinged at the bottom and the V-shaped flap piece was fastened to the steel girth just above her hips with a small padlock. There was a small opening in the front so she could go to the john.

A. J. whistled through his teeth. "I never would have believed a stunt like this. You got a mean daddy, girl."

He stood up and gave her another serious look. "What's your name, sweetheart?"

"Ivoe Thlart."

"Come again."

"Ivoe Thlart."

"OK. You just wait right there." He moved up to the front of the bus looking for some tools. There was a drawer in the stove but it was locked. A heavy box on the floor that looked like it might contain some tools was also locked. A. J. started back down the bus toward one of the windows.

Ivoe said: "You gonna turn me luth?"

A. J. grinned. "You dang whistlin'."

A. J. came back from the river carrying a pair of needle-nose pliers and a couple of fishhooks. Pierpont was right behind him, wheezing slightly as he ran.

"Don't go messing with that. Fools rush in."

A. J. took Pierpont by the shoulders. "Maybe you didn't hear me. There's a girl in that bus, old buddy, and she's tied up with a chain and she's wearing a chastity belt. I got to set her loose before he gets back."

"Who's 'he'?"

"She said her daddy rigged it up."

"Leave it alone, Kid."

A. J. climbed in the window and Pierpont peeked around the corner. Ivoe hadn't moved. She was still naked except for that shiny pair of pants. Pierpont turned away from the window and said: "Oh, Lord!"

A. J. went to work first on the padlock on the stove. He bent the fishhook with the pliers and then inserted it into the lock. He probed around inside until he found the trip bar.

Carefully, he pulled it back with the hook and tripped the latch.

"Hey!" Ivoe said admiringly.

Next, he went to work on the other padlock and pried and twisted it open with the pliers. He severed the chain with the cutters on the pliers and helped Ivoe out of the chastity belt. He pitched it aside and it made a tinny, th-wang sound when it hit the floor, like a beer can on concrete.

Ivoe stood there ummmming and ahhhhing over how good it felt to be out of the thing. A. J. joggled her behind to make sure the circulation was all right. It seemed OK. Then he put the chain and the heavier padlock in his pocket.

"You thure are good with them padlocks," Ivoe said.

A. J. shrugged. "Well, it was easy. That daddy of yours should have bought himself a combination lock. If you ask me, it's a case of being pennywise and dollar foolish." And then he led her to the back of the bus.

Later, Ivoe said: "You thure are nith." Then she giggled. "Won't daddy be mad. Won't he be just awful mad!"

"Your daddy's a preacher, huh?"

Ivoe nodded. "He sells thoap, too." She pointed to all the boxes up front. "And whithkey. Some."

"By the way, where is your daddy?"

"Down there to the river. You didn't see him, huh?"

"No."

There was a tapping on the window shade, and A. J. heard Pierpont outside.

"Psssst. Someone's coming, Kid!"

A. J. said: "Well, I've done about all I can for you, girl. It was nice visiting."

"Who was that?" Ivoe asked.

"Just a friend of mine." A. J. was putting on his clothes.

Her eyes narrowed. "Daddy won't like that either."

Outside, another voice called out: "Ivoe. I'm back."

"That's daddy," Ivoe said and smiled. She was making no attempt to get dressed.

A. J. said: "Maybe you ought to put something on."

"Feels so good like this. I hate them iron pants."

53

"Yeah." A. J. stepped to the window and cracked the shade. There was a big guy out there carrying a stringer of fish. He had a heavy shock of black hair and long ears and muscular arms. Pierpont was nowhere in sight.

The man called out again. "Ivoe? Your daddy's home. Everything all right in there?"

"Everything's juth fine, daddy." And she giggled.

A. J. moved quickly to the front of the bus, but the door was locked on the outside. He moved back toward the rear and was just about to take his chances going out a window, when the shade was ripped back. J. C. Wright peered in.

"Who the hell are you?" he said. And then he saw Ivoe. "God damn!"

"Howdy, preacher," A. J. said. "I was just on my way out."

"Stay where you are!" Then he said: "No you don't. You haul your ass out this window like you got in."

"Well, if you say so." He started to climb out.

Rev. Wright pitched the stringer of fish to one side and ducked under the bus. When he straightened up, he was holding a crowbar over his shoulder, like a baseball bat. "Come on!" he said.

A. J. had no choice. The reverend could have splintered his leg with that crowbar. A. J. dropped to the ground.

"Nice bus you got there."

The reverend swung for A. J.'s head. He missed by an inch, maybe less, and swung again, this time down, and the hook of the bar tore a hole in the side of the bus. Ivoe was standing in the window. Still naked. She squealed and clapped her hands.

"You got here too late this time, daddy!"

The reverend raised the crowbar. A. J. was backed up to the bus. Then Ivoe screamed.

"Look out, daddy. Therth's another one."

Pierpont had come out of hiding in the trees and was trying to sneak up behind Reverend Wright. The preacher swung again, and A. J. dodged to one side. Pierpont shouted:

"Here, Kid. Use this!" And he tossed him the blackjack.

The reverend's eyes flashed and turned into tiny coals. "You son of a bitch!" he said.

He faked a swing and moved in closer. A. J. was dancing on his toes with his back to the bus. The preacher faked again and then swung, and the bar crashed into the side of the bus. The force of the blow threw him slightly off balance and A. J. had an opening to hit him with the blackjack. The first sock sent the reverend to his knees and the second put him out cold.

Ivoe knelt at the window and looked down at the reverend.

"Ooooo!" she said. "Daddy's got a buthted head." Then her eyes became slit and hostile. "And I thought you were nith," she said to A. J.

"Oh, Lord," Pierpont said. "Oh, good Lord!"

A. J. OPENED the door at the motel to Fulton County sheriff deputies Bert Mosler and Charlie McKnight, and Bert said:

"A. J. Poole? The one they call the Watermelon Kid?"

"That's me."

"We got a complaint against you signed by a Reverend Wright. Says you raped his daughter, Ivoe, and assaulted him with a blackjack. We've got a warrant for your arrest." Bert looked at Pierpont. "That must be the other one. What's your name, mister?"

"Pierpont Higgins."

"Better search him, Mac. And look around the room." Bert motioned to A. J. "Turn around, Kid. I got to frisk you."

He found the blackjack first. "This your blackjack?"

A. J. said it was and told Pierpont to keep quiet.

"Blackjacks are illegal, Kid." He found the chain and padlock next and turned A. J. around.

"OK," Bert said. "You can have a seat there now. Let's talk about this a minute. As we understand it, this chain and lock were fastened to this Miss Slart, the reverend's daughter. According to the reverend's complaint, you picked this here lock and cut this chain which was, I believe, welded to this, uh, chastity belt the victim was wearing. Then you forcibly entered this young woman . . ."

A. J. laughed. "Forcibly entered?"

Bert studied him seriously. "You fucked her, didn't you?"

"Well, yeah."

"That's what counts. She was sixteen. Two months shy of her seventeenth birthday. Did you know that?"

"Unh uh. She looks older."

Bert smiled and his lower lip quivered a little. "She does at

56

that. Look, Kid, there could be extenuating circumstances here. You ain't trying to hide. We found you too easy, through your pickup. Trouble is, looks like you did assault that preacher and you were carrying a concealed weapon and that girl ain't but sixteen. But like I say, extenuating circumstances. We heard about this Rev. Wright. He ain't no lily of the valley, and you could have been defending yourself. My thinking is you might get a judge to reduce the charges to statutory rape if you was to enter a plea of guilty and get off with a year, maybe less, on the farm."

Pierpont stepped forward, shoulders back, ready for the firing squad. Confession was written on his face. It was his blackjack. He was an accomplice. He would go to jail, to the ends of the earth, to the moon for A. J. Poole, who had, after all, saved his life. He raised his hand to speak, but A. J. reached out and lowered it.

"I need you on the outside," A. J. whispered and then said to Bert:

"Care for a beer? Got some on ice back there in the sink."

"Falstaff," Mac reported.

Bert said: "Better not. We're on duty. You go ahead though, before we go to town."

"I think I will."

Judge Bobby MacDaggle set A. J.'s bail at $500. The next morning, Pierpont left Mammoth Spring and drove straight to DeValls. He carried the combination to A. J.'s safe.

"Take five hundred and try to make it back here before dark," A. J. had told him.

But when Pierpont got to the house, the bedroom had been turned upside down and the safe was open. There were some powder marks on the bedcovers and wall. Pierpont found a few pennies on the floor and some property deeds, but that was all.

"Son of a bitch!" Pierpont said.

He went up the hill to find Alvin, and Alvin said:

"The Kid's been robbed."

"I know it. I just came from the house."

"You looked at the boat dock, too? They took all the motors and rods and the bait cards. I've been trying to reach you since yesterday."

"The Kid is in jail."

Alvin blinked. "Jail? Shit, man, why?"

"Rape and assault. Up in Mammoth Spring. He needs $500 for bail."

Alvin opened the register. There was about $60 in the till. He gave it to Pierpont.

Pierpont picked up the phone and called A. J. The cop at the station said A. J. was not taking calls. He chuckled.

Pierpont stiffened. "Sir," he said, "this is Congressman Pierpont Higgins from Ohio speaking."

"Which?"

Pierpont repeated it and went on. "Mr. Poole is a personal friend of mine. I demand to speak to him at once."

There was a short silence on the phone and then the cop hung up.

"It didn't work," Pierpont said and looked at Alvin. "I am going to find Leroy."

Leroy was staying at the Starlight Motel in Lepanto. He called a conference of the band and between them they had about $300. They went over to see Flossie and she made up the difference. Then Flossie reached down into the coldbox and hauled up a couple of six packs of Falstaff. "He'll want some beer when he gets out of the pokey."

Pierpont's eyes were watery. He reached out and took Flossie's hand. He squeezed tightly and he was using both hands.

It was about seven o'clock when Pierpont got back to Mammoth Spring. He told A. J. he had raised the money and then about the robbery.

"They cleaned you out, Kid. They really did."

"You say they took the motors, too?"

Pierpont nodded. "But you'll be out on bail first thing in the morning."

Pierpont spent the night in the pickup on the street in front of City Hall. He didn't sleep and kept his eyes on the light in the jailhouse all night long.

The next day Judge MacDaggle set A. J.'s trial for July 17 and let him out on bail.

Jim Bob Brady from DeValls was A. J.'s lawyer. Jim Bob was twenty-six, and he was a serious young man. People said he was a smart lawyer and Jim Bob said: "That's right."

He looked at A. J. They were sitting in Leroy's room at the Starlight. The boys were lined up against the wall. Leroy sat beside A. J. Pierpont was over by the window pulling on his goatee.

Jim Bob said: "Kid, you're going to spend a little time in jail, and that's all there is to it. I wish I could keep you out but I can't. I intend to plead you guilty to statutory rape and aggravated assault."

There was some restlessness in the room, and Jim Bob raised his hand for silence. He went on. "The judge will appreciate that. I did a little checking into this MacDaggle, and people up there say he hates long trials. Gets meaner the longer they last. So, we're going to keep this short and sweet. My guess is MacDaggle will give you six months to a year, and you'll be on your way to Tucker Prison within twenty-four hours after the trial. That's the best I can do for you."

Pierpont said angrily: "You call that a defense?"

"Easy, Higgins," Jim Bob said. "None of that is important. What is is this." He hesitated a moment. There was not a sound in the room. Jim Bob looked at A. J. "Do you know any judo?"

A. J. was a little surprised. "They taught us some there during Korea. I never got too handy at it."

"What the hell, Jim Bob?"

"Take it easy, Thurmond," Leroy said. "Let Jim Bob talk."

"Jim Bob's got the floor," Will said.

"Now's the time," Jim Bob told A. J. "Tucker is a bad place. Rough. Now, you've got close to two months before your case comes up. You can learn a lot in that time. There's a guy I know in Forrest City. Name of Johnny Burkart. Johnny's an expert. He got brown belts and black belts and I've seen a belt he's got that has rhinestones on it. If you want to learn judo, Johnny's the best. And get him to tell you about something new he picked up in Japan. It's called Karachi or that's close. I've seen how it works. Johnny takes two two-by-fours and lays them between piles of bricks and he can break them both clean in two with one chop, like that, of his bare hand."

"No lie?" A. J. said.

"No lie."

"Not a bad idea, Kid," Leroy said.

Jim Bob said: "Meanwhile, you got to go in training."

"Training?"

"Sure. Push-ups. Chin-ups. Sit-ups. Laps."

"Laps?"

"The works. Just like in the Army. Only you've really got to get in shape this time. You've got yourself a gut there. Too much high living. Too much beer. But you'll strip that off running two miles a day."

"Aw, come on, Jim Bob," A. J. said.

Jim Bob scowled. He took A. J. by the shoulders. "I shit you not. I'm talking about one of the meanest prisons in the nation. Fights. Murders. Male rape. Guys getting their throats slit in their beds. Fourteen hours a day on the asphalt gang when it's a hundred in the shade. And that Tucker Telephone. They wire it up to your balls and it feels like the Fourth of July between your legs when the call comes through. You don't want that Tucker Telephone. No sir. But you got to be ready for anything. I've seen guys go in there baby-faced and clean, and when they got out, they had more scars on their faces than a cueball."

He paused and slapped A. J.'s knee. "So, you start in training tomorrow. Chins and push-ups. Twenty-five each and work up to fifty a day. Same with the laps. You start with a mile and work up to two, maybe three miles a day. Hell, why not four? When you're ready, you'll be in better shape than Marciano. And just as tough."

"If I ain't dead before I'm sent up."

"Cut the joking, Kid. This is serious."

Leroy said the Highway 70 Six would help because A. J. would need company and encouragement during the long period of training. And competition would give him something to measure his progress by. The boys agreed, and every morning in front of the Starlight and after they moved over to Marked Tree, everybody, even Pierpont, turned out for an hour of exercises and running.

Doodle Socket took part for one day and then said he had better things to do than run his ass off. Pierpont quit after three weeks, but he had lost twenty pounds. He looked good. Then Pepper dropped out, saying all that sweat was no good for his acne. Rainbow had her baby (around the middle of June) and came back with the band. She joined the training camp and pushed and chinned with the rest of them. Rainbow said it was good for her figure.

Leroy and Thurmond stayed until the first week in July when they said the running was getting them down. That left Rainbow and Will, who finally pulled out one morning, panting at the St. Francis River bridge at the end of the third mile. A. J. had kept running.

Three days a week, A. J. drove down to Forrest City for his judo lessons with Johnny Burkart. Jim Bob kept tabs on him by calling Johnny every Saturday morning for a progress report. One morning a few days before the trial, Johnny said:

"It's wild, Jim Bob. The Kid's great. Another couple of weeks and he'd be as good as me. And that's good, Jim Bob."

"I believe you."

A. J. had never looked better. His body was tanned and as lean as a sirloin strip. And the night before the trial, he got a surprise.

A. J. was alone in his room when he heard a knock on the door. He opened it, and Rainbow was standing there in a raincoat and it wasn't raining. She came into the room and slipped the raincoat off her shoulders. She had on one of the prettiest, lowest-cut nightgowns of pure white satin you ever saw.

A. J. was about to say something, but Rainbow put a finger to her lips. Then she ran her hands over her thighs and up the front of her gown, slowly, softly. She smiled and said:

"Leroy knows. It's something special. Very special, for your last night."

"Come here, baby."

She moved toward him. A. J. took her in his arms and lifted her clear off the floor and then laid her down on the bed.

"I've waited a long time for this," Rainbow said, and her eyes were closed.

A. J.'s trial lasted one day. On July 18 at 10 o'clock in the morning, Judge MacDaggle looked at the prisoner standing before the bar and handed down his sentence: Two years on the prison farm at Tucker, Arkansas, on the charge of statutory rape, one year suspended; one year on the charge of aggravated assault, six months suspended. Both sentences to be served concurrently.

Jim Bob raised his arms over his head, his hands clasped in a victory salute. Then he reached over and pounded A. J. on the back.

"A year, old buddy. That's light. About what I figured, but you'll be out in less on good behavior. I told you we'd be all right if we kept it short and sweet." He looked at A. J. and smiled sincerely. "Well, you're on your way, Kid. You'll be at the farm tonight. Remember. It's a rough place, but you're ready. You can hack it."

A. J. said: "Jim Bob, you're one hell of a lawyer."

Jim Bob hesitated a moment. He wasn't quite sure how A. J. meant that. Then Jim Bob punched him lightly on the shoulder and grinned. "You know it, Kid."

A. J.'s bunk was on the south side of Barracks #216 and through the bars he could see one of the okra fields, in the center of which was an elm tree where the guards stood in the shade in the summertime. Left, out of the window was another barracks and to the right of that the main building where the warden had his office. A fence with slanted barbed wire at top surrounded the compound.

The bunk on A. J.'s left was empty but John Ed Rowland occupied the one on his right. John Ed was medium-sized, about 170–175 pounds, but he was psychotic, and if he had known it, he wouldn't have cared. He was serving a twenty-year term for murder and he admired men and women who were killed in the electric chair. His head was flat on top and his hair was bushy and his eyes were close-set and small and grey.

The second night A. J. was in prison, John Ed came over and put his foot on A. J.'s bunk.

"Your name's Poole. The one they call the Watermelon Kid."

"That's me," A. J. smiled.

"How come they call you that?"

"I can eat a lot of watermelon."

"You look like a cocksucker to me."

A. J. got off the bed. Everybody in the barracks was quiet and watching. Dekker, the guard in the cage down at the end of the barracks, said nothing. He was eating a peanut butter sandwich and sliced cucumbers.

"I might fool you," A. J. said.

John Ed was very quick. His knees bent into a crouch and his right hand, fingers pointed, shot out aiming for that soft spot at the diaphragm just under the rib cage. A. J. blocked it, took John Ed's arm and with his hip flipped him completely over. John Ed came down face-first on the floor and let out a cry.

A. J. moved out into the center of the room and waited for him to get up. John Ed moved on the floor like a snake, his arms and legs outstretched and reaching to support himself from the floor. When he got to his feet, his eyes were wide and crazy. And then he lunged. A. J. chopped him down and John Ed hit the floor with a grunt. But he was not through. He sprang again and tackled A. J., but as they fell, A. J. flipped him over with his feet and pushed him through the doorway into the head. John Ed tumbled and slid across the floor and his head came to rest in front of the toilet bowl. A. J. went in and pulled him out by the legs and dropped him on the floor of the barracks. It was over.

The other men had watched in silence. Dekker had finished his sandwich and the cucumbers. He leaned back chewing the last mouthful and raised his feet to the desk and opened a magazine. A. J. sat down on his bunk and looked at the other men. A couple of them saluted with a finger and a few shrugged. Talking started up again.

A big, hairy man in an undershirt who had gargantuan arms and a crooked chin came down the center aisle and stopped at A.J.'s bunk. With him was a little man with quick, nervous eyes and smooth skin. The big man said:

"You handle yourself pretty good, Kid. My name's Woodrow Mason. This here," he motioned to the other man, "is Rudy Blaylock. Rudy might do you some good."

"I'd be obliged then."

"John Ed over there," Woodrow said, "sure as Pete's going to get himself killed one of these days. I wish you'd done it. You don't have to be a psychiatrist to know he's crazy. What I mean is, he won't let you alone now. He'll be laying for you. One night, you'll be sleeping there and he'll sneak over and slit your throat like an orange. That's where Rudy comes in."

A.J. looked at Rudy and Rudy nodded.

"Rudy can't sleep," Woodrow said. "Got insomnia bad. So what some of us do—I do it myself—is to take care of Rudy and Rudy keeps an eye on things at night. You can sleep safe as long as you got Rudy for a lookout."

"Don't you ever sleep?" A.J. asked Rudy.

"Very light," Woodrow said. "He's wide awake at a footstep. He can hear a pin dròp." Woodrow took out a pouch of tobacco and paper and began rolling a cigarette. "You haven't asked what it's going to cost you."

"What then?"

"Cigarettes. Candy. Every once in a while we get a little Mary Jane in here, and Rudy's crazy about a joint. And script. Whatever you can spare or feel it's worth." Woodrow smiled.

"Sounds like pretty cheap insurance to me."

"That's right." Woodrow sat down on the vacant bunk. "I can see you're wondering about Rudy. Well, he's dumb." Woodrow nodded. "Can't talk a word. A grunt or two and Rudy's said it. That's why he hears so well. You lose one sense and the others get stronger. It shouldn't have happened to Rudy, though. You won't believe this, but once upon a time Rudy was a singer. That's right. Sung for a living, he did. Roadhouse bands and even on the radio. Made good money, too. People knew Rudy Blaylock and they liked to hear him sing."

"What happened?"

"Ran out of money and knocked over a liquor store in Shreveport. Fellow got shot and Rudy got sent to Angola Prison. That's where it happened. You can't keep a bird in a cage. One night he broke out. Him and another guy. They got caught, though, and they put Rudy in the box. When they brought him out later, somebody had cut his vocal cords. Couldn't talk. Couldn't sing. Couldn't tell who did it and he never learned to read nor write so nobody knows."

He scruffed the back of Rudy's neck and laughed. "Rudy don't mind any more. He's a born lookout, and he's crazy about the radio. Got one of his own over there by his bunk. Can't sing a note of music but he loves to hear it." Woodrow paused and drew on his cigarette. "There's something else you might care to know. I'm a little older than the rest of the guys in here and the others kind of look to me as their leader." He ground out his cigarette and looked at A. J. with a hard smile. "John Ed tried me once."

A. J. put up his hands. "Man, I am not looking for trouble. All I want is to get out of here as fast as I can."

"Well, you can't hurry it, Kid. You'll do your time."

"How long you in for?"

"Life."

Lights went out at nine o'clock. The guard turned in in the cage and there was a yellow night light on beside his cot. The light from this spilled out over the far end of the barracks and seemed stuck like dingy yellow paper to the ceiling. The moon was full. It had risen half way in the eastern sky, and in its light the bars slanted across the bunks and floor and broke against the walls.

A. J. could not go right to sleep. He looked over at John Ed, who was lying on his side facing the other way. His legs were curled under him and his head was buried in the mattress. Every once in a while a leg would strike out convulsively at the foot of his bed and then be still.

A. J. looked beyond John Ed. He could see the glow from the tubes in the radio beside Rudy's bunk. Rudy was awake. His head was down close to the radio and he had it turned on very low. A. J. strained to make out the music. It was Bobby

Pickett again singing "The Love Sick Blues." And Rudy was lying there, his fingers pressed against his jaw, and his mouth was working fast and furiously and the veins were standing out in his neck. But he wasn't making a sound. A shudder passed through A. J.'s body. His hands were wet, and at the back of his neck and under his arms he was sweating profusely.

Jim Bob and Pierpont came to see A. J. on the first visiting Sunday, and Jim Bob said:

"Whipped anybody with that judo yet?"

A. J. told them about the fight.

"Hot damn!" Jim Bob's eyes were flashing.

"They call me Mr. Moto."

"You'll do all right. You'll do fine."

Pierpont looked guilty. "That was my blackjack, Kid. I ought to be here the same as you."

Jim Bob spoke up. "Pierpont, you wouldn't last an hour. Right, Kid?"

A. J. smiled. "You're always right, Jim Bob."

"How's the food, Kid?" Pierpont said.

"Don't ask him about that, Pierpont," Jim Bob said. "The food's terrible."

Pierpont spoke up hotly. "That's right, Jim Bob!"

Jim Bob shrugged. "Well, hell, it is."

A. J. said: "How's Leroy and them. Rainbow OK?"

"Fine. Everybody's fine. They'll be down to see you soon. Look, Kid," Pierpont went on, "if there is anything I can do."

"Well, you can slip me five bucks if you've got it. I owe a guy something. But look out the guard don't see."

Pierpont gave him the money and Jim Bob said: "We'll be going. Stay loose, Kid. Keep in there."

"Thanks, Jim Bob."

Leroy and the others came to see him every month or so and one time early in December they staged an impromptu concert in the yard. It was a big success. Everybody was crazy about Doodle Socket, but it was Rainbow just walking around that drove the inmates wild.

Rudy loved the show most of all. During one of Doodle's

numbers, Rudy stood up with his hands over his head, reaching, shut his eyes and started swaying and mouthing the words to the song. His head was raised, and if you had been close to him, you could have heard just the faintest whisper of air, but it wasn't close to music.

After the concert, A. J. told Pierpont: "There's something I want you to get for me." Some other people were standing around and A. J. whispered in his ear. "Think you can find it? Might be kind of hard."

Pierpont said sure.

"No hurry. Just so you get it to me before I get out."

Winter passed. In March A. J. got a letter from Rainbow. She was pregnant again and due in May. She closed the letter by saying: "It's that son of a bitch, Leroy again. Wish it was you."

A. J. got another letter in March, this time from Jim Bob. Jim Bob told him he was being considered for early release on good behavior. "Take it easy, Kid. Stay loose." The next day the warden called A. J. into his office and made it official. He'd be freed in April. A. J. left the office walking on his toes.

Every time Pierpont had come to see him, A. J. reminded him about that special project. Pierpont had said he was working on it and needed a little more time. Then a couple of weeks before A. J. got out, Pierpont showed up carrying a small, flat package. "I had a hard time finding one, Kid. Had to send off for it."

"Good man. Good man." A. J. took the package over to the guard and unwrapped it so the guard could see. The guard looked it over a minute, then nodded OK. Later that afternoon A. J. tucked the package under his mattress. No one else was in the barracks at the time.

That night there was a stir in the dining room. The word was passed along: Rudy Blaylock and Woodrow had broken out. It had happened when they had gone into town with Stephens, one of the guards. They had knocked Stephens out and stolen the truck. But the truck had already been found, on the other side of Pine Bluff, and the tank was empty.

"I didn't know a thing about it," A. J. said.

"Nobody else either," Larry Apple, the guy eating next to him said: "It was a hell of a secret."

Outside, they could hear the dogs barking.

Two days went by. Three. Then the word passed again. Woodrow and Rudy had been caught. The night before, and Woodrow was in the box.

"What about Rudy?" A. J. asked.

"There's rumors," Apple said. "Some say he's in the box with Woodrow. But Dekker says he saw 'em put Woodrow in and Rudy wasn't with him. I don't know. Bet we seen the last of Rudy."

The next morning the prison warden officially announced Rudy's death. A. J. learned of it from Dekker.

"He was shot four times," Dekker said. "Blew his head clean off."

"Who shot him?"

"Who cares?"

A. J. went to his bunk and sat down. Apple came down the aisle. He looked at A. J. and said: "Rudy would have been twenty-five years old this Friday."

"Yeah, I know," A. J. said and reached under his mattress. He pulled out the package and opened it. It contained a tiny radio made with something new called transistors. It came with a loop so you could carry it on a belt and had a wire and an earplug. A. J. took the radio over to Rudy's bunk and set it on the floor. And he turned it on and put the volume up as high as it would go.

Nine months to the day he entered prison, on April 15, 1956, A. J. was released from Tucker, and Pierpont was there to meet him.

"You look great, Kid. Really great."

"Let's get out of here."

They stopped in Stuttgart and bought two six packs of Falstaff, and A. J. finished the first can before they were out of town. Then they stopped at a butcher shop and A. J. had the man cut him a three-inch sirloin that was a foot long. A. J. got back in the car, smelling the steak and Pierpont handed him an open beer. A. J. put his knees on the dash and said: "Drive slow, Pierpont, I want to enjoy this ride."

Pierpont filled him in on DeValls. Alvin and the restaurant were doing fine. He (Pierpont) had taken over the management of the boat dock and they had made $300 in the last month. He looked at A. J. proudly.

"You're a good man, Pierpont."

"I told you I had business sense."

They drove on in silence for a while and then Pierpont said: "Do you want to talk about it?"

"What?"

"Back there."

"Oh, there ain't too much to say."

"Why did you want that radio?"

"It was for a friend of mine. He was crazy about music. I owed him some favors. He never got the radio."

"What happened?"

"They shot him when he tried to escape."

After a pause, Pierpont said: "What else did you do back there?"

"Picked a lot of okra."

Pierpont looked at A. J. thoughtfully. "Prison is a hard life."

"Let me tell you."

7

LEROY WAS SITTING at the bar in Thurlo and Mae May-
field's tavern in Berry City working on his second beer. It
was a midafternoon early in July. He was worried and looked
it. He faced a couple of problems, and one was the telegram
from Rainbow that Pepper had just handed him. She was in
West Memphis.

Leroy studied the wire. It read:

> WAS SNATCHED LAST NIGHT   STOP
> THEY WON'T LET ME SAY WHAT I WANT
> STOP   WAS RAPED TWICE   STOP   TWO
> I DIDN'T KNOW   STOP   SUSPECT ONE
> NIGGER   STOP   OUT OF CLOTHES AND
> BEER   ADVISE
>
>   RAINBOW

Will and Thurmond came into the bar and Leroy showed
them the telegram. "I don't know if she's serious or not,"
Leroy said.

"What's she doing in West Memphis?" Will said.

"Who knows? She went over there once with Doodle
Socket to see his agent. Maybe she went back. I haven't laid
eyes on her since Sunday."

"It's Friday afternoon," Thurmond said.

"I know it."

Leroy pondered the matter. Rainbow had been acting funny
lately. Maybe weird was a better word. Ever since her second
child, Clint, had been born. She'd taken off one other time
with no notice and had been gone for three days. She had
generally been full of bullshit and wildness. Maybe the wire
was just a gag, but maybe it was the truth. So Leroy wrote
out a wire and told Pepper to send it. It read:

GET A BUS TONIGHT. AM
SENDING $5. TAKE IT EASY.
FONDLY.

LEROY

Pepper went out with the money and Leroy said: "Where the hell is Doodle Socket, anyway?"

"He's watching that flagpole sitter again," Thurmond said.

"Well, go see what he's up to. I don't want him hanging on the pole like he did the other night and get arrested for disturbing the peace. I had a hard time talking that cop out of running him in."

Homer Skipsingle was Leroy's other problem. Homer was no ordinary polesitter, the kind who wandered up the valley every few years looking for eats and maybe fifty bucks. No. Homer was a professional. He was serious about it. He held the record in Kansas City of sixty-eight days on the pole in Memorial Park, and any record anywhere Homer considered a challenge.

There wasn't a record in Cherokee County to speak of. There had been a couple of flagpole sitters over the years who had tried the pole in the little park across the street from the Manningham-Becker Department Store, but they had come down after a day or so and no one had bothered to keep any records or even remember their names. There was a record for Arkansas, though, of twenty-four days, set by a man from Tallahassee, Florida, in Little Rock back in 1938. Twenty-four days. Nothing to Homer, but it was a record to break.

Why?

"Because it's there."

Homer had tremendous style. He would not just sit on his platform on top of the pole. He also sang and danced. He danced fast and he could swing. He played the banjo and he was pretty good, and he sang fairly well in a tenor voice. Homer was a little man, light on his feet, and he had long, hairy arms some people said made him look like a monkey and which all agreed were good for climbing. And he had a narrow, curled moustache and half-slit, crafty eyes.

71

Homer made a deal with Mr. Manningham and Mr. Becker, and the deal was that Homer would set a new state record right there in the park across from the department store and the stunt would draw a crowd on a continuing basis. That crowd, naturally, would wander into the store and sales would boom. Homer's contract was for a minimum of twenty-five days for $300 plus food and drink. The $300 would be written off as advertising.

Mr. Manningham didn't believe he could do it and didn't like paying $300 in advance but he said all right when Homer showed him a certificate of appreciation he'd received from Mayor Bill Ruben in Kansas City, Missouri, and a copy of the photograph of Homer and Bill when they awarded him the key to the city on the morning of the sixty-ninth day. Homer would not have come down then if it hadn't been for a series of violent storms that moved into Kansas and Missouri. Even so, they had to beg him to quit. He had wanted to stay up there for at least a hundred days.

So far, Homer had been on top of the pole in Berry City for ten days, and he wasn't tired or afraid or bothered by a thing. He was on radio station KBEQ every morning and gave the weather report. He hauled up the mike with a rope and pulley and broadcast live for sixty seconds. People heard him as far away as Dallas and Des Moines and he closed the broadcast humming and singing a little of Cole Porter's "Blue Skies."

He gave a show at eleven in the morning and then again at two and four and 5:30 and 7:30 and a late show at nine. The fire department cooperated with the store and turned a spotlight on him for the twilight and after-dark shows. A man from the Ed Sullivan Show called and said Ed wanted to talk to him when Homer passed the twenty-fifth day. Homer said fine. At night he slept as soundly as a baby curled up on his platform. Homer was one of the best small sleepers in the country. He'd brag that he could sleep anywhere in any position and said that once he'd slept twelve hours straight in a number 4 washtub to win a five-dollar bet.

Berry City loved him. The park was crawling with people all day and for the shows at night. A carnival man heard about him and moved in with a small tilt-a-whirl and three ponies and tried to sell rides in the park. But Homer sent a note to Mayor Sam Norman, and Sam ran him out of town. Homer wanted a one-man show. So did Manningham and Becker. The store was doing a fast business and they looked forward to record sales for weeks, for months. Homer was talking about not only a new state record but a national record and maybe even a world record, which was somewhere around 209 days held by a man in India.

Ed Jones's Domino and Pool Parlor half a block down the street from the department store was doing a land office business. Ed was a skinny, sleepy-eyed man who was as pale as a mushroom and wore dark glasses. Over the years his trade had been slow but steady. Pool was a nickel a game; snooker and dominoes a dime, beer was fifteen cents for a glass of Schlitz from the tap and he drew a nickel every time Early Williams snapped out a fifteen-cent shine.

Now, Ed was going to town. His bar was packed with guys buying beer before and after each of Homer's shows, and Ed upped the price to twenty cents. He ordered in several gross of paper cups so they could take it out and he made a small fortune on Cheez-its and peanuts. Before Homer, Ed was selling a keg of beer a week but now he was doing twice that in a single day, and at twenty cents a glass that was something. He took off his dark glasses and smiled at his customers and there was a flush of rose in his cheeks.

But what was good for business uptown was killing it down by the river at Thurlo and Mae's tavern. Beer and set-up sales were off by an amazing 60 percent, according to Mae, who kept good figures. The jukebox had brought in only $2 in nickels in a week, and the $75 a night they were paying for the Highway 70 Six to entertain crowds of six or seven on a good night was money down the drain, flushed, gone, good-bye.

Mae had spoken to Thurlo and Thurlo had spoken to Leroy and that was what had Leroy worried. If Homer stayed up on that pole much longer, the band's engagement was going to be canceled and Thurlo and Mae would close and go fishing for the duration. You couldn't top an act like Homer's and there was no point in trying. Thurlo knew when he was licked.

And worst of all, the weather had been perfect. Not a drop of rain or a whisper of thunder in weeks and none in the forecast, short or extended. Leroy looked outside the window, through which the sun was streaming, warm and cheery. It blazed on the Wassekia River bridge and beat down on the streets which were as dry and white as bones.

"God damn that son of a bitching Homer Skipsingle," Leroy said. "I wish the Kid was here."

At that moment, A. J. and Pierpont walked into the bar.

It was almost dark. Homer Skipsingle was sitting in the spotlight on the pole above City Park with his legs dangling in rhythm over the side and he was playing and singing "Roll Me Up Cornbread Mama 'Cause I Wanna Get Fried." The crowd was loving it. The people stamped their feet, and even the toes of the old-timers on the park benches tapped to the beat. There was a steady flow of men in and out of Ed's billiard and domino parlor carrying cups, some empty and some full, and from the full ones sudsy beer splashed on the sidewalk.

When Homer finished "Cornbread Mama," he stood up on his platform and went into a jig, still strumming furiously on his banjo. Then he fell to his knees with his eyes closed and playing so hard it was a wonder the strings didn't start to smoke, and he ended up with a yell so wild it sounded like a Comanche in the act of scalping a minister. The men and women hollered and clapped and the kids shouted gleefully.

"I see what you mean," A. J. said to Leroy, who could hardly hear him over the applause.

They were standing on the curb in front of Ed's drinking beer. They had just watched Homer's 7:30 show. "He's got some act," A. J. said.

Doodle Socket sneered. "It's that flagpole gimmick that does the trick. He can't sing worth a shit." Doodle Socket hated him more than the others.

"You ought to see him pull his teetering act," Will said.

74

"He finishes up with a little twist, steps back and looks like he's going to fall. His legs swing way out and he's pumping to keep his balance. Just barely manages to catch himself."

"I wish he'd bust his ass," Doodle Socket said.

"It's his eleventh day up there," Thurmond put in.

"We need to think this through," A. J. said and started down the street for Thurlo's.

Pierpont fell into step beside him. His tone was cautious. "What is your thinking, Kid?"

"I don't know. Homer's tough competition."

"I wish to remind you of one thing, Kid," Pierpont said. "You got out of prison two months ago."

Rainbow was waiting for them at the tavern when they came in. Her suitcase was up on the table, and she was sitting in the chair with her legs crossed perfectly. Thurlo, behind the bar, was trying to listen to the news on the radio and keep an eye on Rainbow's legs at the same time, and he wasn't getting much of the news.

A couple of regular customers who didn't care for Homer were down at the end of the bar where they could look at Rainbow. They froze every time she made a move. The rest of the stools and tables were empty.

A. J. and Pierpont and the others sat at the bar and let Leroy and Rainbow have a private talk.

Leroy moved over to her table and said: "Well, I see you made it."

"Yeah. Thanks for the five bucks, big spender."

Leroy motioned to the suitcase. He was suspicious. "You got your things there."

"The cops found it."

"Look here, Rainbow. Was that wire a gag or what?"

Rainbow whipped her legs open and snatched up her dress. "Here! You want to inspect?" she said between her teeth.

Leroy stepped quickly to shield her from the eyes at the bar. "God damn, Rainbow, this is a public place!"

Rainbow put her dress back down and re-crossed her legs. "You watch what you say then."

"OK. OK. So what happened?"

"I don't want to talk about it."

"All right then." He motioned to the others and everybody came over and pulled up chairs to have a conference about Homer. They filled Rainbow in, and Pierpont said:

"Whatever you do, it must be legal."

"I wish we knew how to make lightning," Doodle Socket said. "What we need is a big, bad, ass-rolling storm. That'd get him down."

"If we could talk to him," Leroy said, "maybe we could make a deal."

"No deals," Doodle Socket said.

"What kind of deal?" Rainbow said.

"We'd have to offer him something," Will said, looking thoughtfully at Rainbow.

"What's this cat look like?" Rainbow said.

"He's short, hairy, and stupid," Doodle Socket said. "You ought to go for him."

Rainbow uncrossed her legs and kicked Doodle Socket under the table.

"God!" Doodle Socket gasped and doubled over.

"Cut it out, Rainbow!" Leroy said.

"Well, make him shut up."

Doodle Socket was still bent over, breathing hard.

Leroy looked at Rainbow. "You could climb that pole and have a talk with Homer."

"Ha!" Rainbow said.

"Maybe you could talk him down, Rainbow," A. J. said.

"No."

"We might take him in with us," Pepper said.

"Nothing doing!" Doodle Socket gasped from under the table. "That's out."

"He wouldn't go for it anyway," A. J. said. "He's doing all right by himself."

They were silent for a while and then A. J. said: "How's this dude take a crap?"

Leroy said: "He uses a bucket. Hauls it up every morning on a rope and he's got a little screen he sits behind. They give him a fresh bucket every morning."

Thurlo came over and stood at the table. His face was serious. Everybody looked at Thurlo and Thurlo shook his head.

76

"Hate to do it," he told Leroy. "But after tomorrow night, you boys will have to look for another place. Can't cut it with Homer in town."

Leroy introduced him to A. J. and said: "Jesus, man, give us a little time. We'll think of something."

Thurlo shrugged. "We might just close down altogether," he said and went back to the bar.

The band had a show at nine o'clock. Thurmond and Will were already on the stand tuning up. Pepper went over to join them and then came running back.

"Wait a minute, Kid, I think I see what you were getting at. We'll sabotage Homer's diet. Right? We'll talk to whoever fixes his food and get them to send him up nothing but Mexican food for a week. Chili and enchiladas and twice-fried beans. And don't forget the peppers. Some of them hot McIlhenny peppers from Louisiana. That'll throw a cake in his program, hey?" Pepper was very excited.

Leroy stood up. "Come on Pepper," he said, "let's go to work."

The band played for an hour. The two guys remained faithfully at the bar, but nobody else came in. Doodle Socket didn't like not having an audience. He sang with a sneer and his moves were lousy. During breaks, the boys all had a beer and sat out at the table. From up the street, they could hear the applause from Homer's late show.

Homer pulled one of his teetering acts at the two o'clock show Saturday afternoon, and in the excitement two women fainted in an azalea bed. When they were brought around, Homer yelled down to them from his platform: "I'm awfully sorry, ladies, I'll be more careful up here after this. I'd hate for anybody to have to go home with a case of the palpitations."

The people all clapped and the two women waved up at Homer and smiled even though they still felt a little weak.

A. J. and Leroy walked slowly back to the tavern. It was Homer's twelfth day, the crowds were getting bigger and the sun was still shining.

A. J. and Leroy sat down with Pierpont, and A. J. made

himself a rum and Coke. A. J. drank slowly and stirred it with the plastic stick. Leroy and Pierpont had beers. Doodle Socket and Rainbow were playing gin rummy at another table and arguing. Thurmond was asleep in a booth. Pepper was across the table eating Mamacita Bullets from Reynosa, and studying his book on pharmacology. The two faithful guys were again at the bar. Will was outside on the deck where the people sometimes danced in the summertime, and he was yodeling, but not too loudly.

A. J. was slumped in his seat. Slowly, he straightened up. He was looking intently at the stirrer in his hand. He motioned to Leroy and fixed the stick firmly between the thumb and index finger on his left hand and with his right he bent back the tip and let it vibrate. He looked at Leroy.

"This give you any ideas, man?"

Leroy was on his feet and his feet were almost dancing. "You bet it does! Get over here, everybody." He tapped on the window. "Will, come in here."

They gathered around and Leroy said: "Show 'em Kid."

A. J. said: "Somebody get me a rubber band." Pepper gave him one, and A. J. said: "See this stick? That's the flagpole. And up here," he tapped the little boob on the end with his finger, "sits Homer on his platform. We find some way, at night, with a rope to bend back that pole, like this." He pulled back the stick with the rubber band. "It'll bend. It's thinner at the top than the bottom. And if old Homer won't cooperate," he let the rubber band loose and it sailed off the table.

"Hot damn!" Will said and everybody cheered.

Pierpont said: "Good God, Kid, we can't do that!"

"It's just a bluff, Pierpont. But it'll work."

"I'll get the rope," Pepper said. "Genuine hemp. We'll need at least a couple of hundred feet." He started for the door. Thurmond went with him.

"I'll take it up," Doodle Socket said. "I can climb."

"How will we bend the pole?" Rainbow said. "Can we all do it?"

A. J. said: "We can use the pickup."

Will shook his head. "It may be stiffer than we think. Play it safe and use a tractor."

Leroy looked at Will. "Can you get us a tractor?"

"One tractor coming up," Will said and headed for the door. Pierpont went after him.

"Where are you going, Pierpont?" A. J. said.

"With Will. He might try to steal it."

That night at the stroke of twelve they were all outside the Sands Motel waiting for Pepper to get back. Will and the tractor were parked on a side street under a large elm tree. Will was smoking a cigar and yodeling softly. Pierpont was standing by the tree, pulling nervously on his goatee. A. J. checked in with them.

"Almost ready," he said, and then looked at Will. "When you come in, come in quiet."

"In a tractor?"

"Well, as quiet as you can." He looked at Pierpont. "Where'd you get this thing?"

"Thurlo's brother owns a farm. Kid, I just thought of something. A tractor like this could tear up that little park."

"Can't be helped," Will said and looked at A. J.

"Don't see how," A. J. said, and went back to the others.

Leroy was handing out flashlights. He looked at Rainbow. "You know what to do if you spot a cop."

Rainbow nodded.

Pepper came stealing out of the shadows across the street like an infantryman under fire.

"Homer's asleep," Pepper said. "Curled up like a puppy."

"We're ready then."

The park was deserted. Homer was asleep on his platform. There were lights at the four corners of the park but the interior was dark except for one light that shined on the face of Stonewall Jackson riding a rearing horse. Thurmond turned the lights off Stonewall and joined Pepper, who was laying out the rope from the base of the flagpole.

A. J. and Leroy were standing on a park bench like generals directing a battle. Rainbow was roaming the streets. Doodle was waiting below the flagpole with the rope in his teeth. Will and the tractor, with Pierpont as a lookout ahead, came up the street behind the park. Will was driving as quiet as he could. He pulled into the park and stopped behind the darkened statue of Stonewall.

The headlights from a prowl car swung into Main Street and swept across the park. Everybody ducked and held their breaths. The cop who was driving turned his spot on Homer's platform. Everything was OK. Then the headlights picked up Rainbow down the street. She was dead center in the middle of the street and was looking back over her shoulder. Then she pulled her legs together, rubbed one against the other and started her walk. Leroy said later it was the high point of her career. The two cops in the car looked at each other and followed when Rainbow turned down a side street. They didn't come back.

A. J. gave the signal. Will pulled into place and Doodle Socket started slowly up the pole.

It only took a couple of minutes. Doodle tied the rope with a bowline just above the struts that supported Homer's platform. He looked down at A. J. and then at Will. The line was secured. Doodle Socket knocked on the underside of the platform and said:

"Wake up, buddy, your time has come."

Homer uncurled, flipped over on his hands and knees and crouched looking wild-eyed into the darkness. Doodle knocked on the platform again, and Homer leaned over the side of the board. He came face to face with Doodle Socket.

"What's going on here? Who the hell are you?"

"Kiss my ass," Doodle Socket said and started down.

At the same time Will put the tractor in reverse and moved slowly, a foot or so. The pole bent and the platform began to tilt slightly.

Homer gripped the sides of the platform and called out: "Hey? Who's out there? What are you trying to pull?"

Everybody turned their flashlights on the rope and the pole and Will switched on the tractor's lights so Homer could see what was going on. Then, everybody turned their lights off and it was dark again.

Leroy looked at A. J. and A. J. called up. "We want to talk to you, Homer."

Homer called back, "You son of a bitch. Who are you?"

"Never mind that. You've got to get out of town."

"The hell you say! I'm staying up here for twenty-five days. Maybe a hundred. I'm under contract."

"Be smart, Homer," Leroy called up.

A. J. signaled to Will and Will moved the tractor back a couple more feet.

"Hey! For Chrissakes. Cut that out!"

"Come on down, Homer," A. J. said.

"No."

Will moved back another foot or two. The platform and Homer were leaning precariously now. Homer was trying to hold on to his banjo and his life, and his knuckles were white.

Doodle Socket stepped over to the taut rope and called up to Homer. "Look what I got here," Doodle said. He turned on his flashlight and held up the knife. Slowly, he started sawing on the hemp.

Pierpont said: "Careful, Doodle Socket. Very careful."

"Come on down, Homer," A. J. said.

"Let him stay," Doodle Socket said. "I'll have this rope cut in a minute, and we'll turn him loose like a kite."

"All right! ALL RIGHT!" Homer shouted. "Ease off that rope. I'm coming down. Don't bend this pole any more. Jesus!"

"That's more like it, Homer," Leroy said.

Will moved forward with the tractor, and the pole righted itself. Homer slung his banjo over his shoulder and came out through a little trapdoor in the platform.

Doodle Socket called up. "Bring the rope down when you come."

"Huh?"

"Untie the rope up there."

"Oh. Yeah." After a moment, the rope fell free.

Will churned up the tractor and got out of there fast. He was driving without lights. He mashed two azalea beds, toppled one fountain, and laid waste one boxwood hedge. Pepper and Thurmond coiled up the rope. They were almost finished when Homer hit the ground.

"Welcome back to earth, Homer," Leroy said.

"You sons a bitches. You sons a bitches!"

"Don't take it like that, Homer," A. J. said. "We're doing you a favor. A man could get killed up there. He could get struck by lightning."

"Or worse," Leroy put in.

"I'll get you for this, you bastards! I'll get the cops."

"Shut up, punk," Doodle Socket said.

"No law's been broken," A. J. said. "You broke your contract, though. Look, Homer, we want to help you. That's right. We've fixed it so you can leave town without the least bit of embarrassment."

"Embarrassment."

"For running out on your contract."

They had closed in a circle around him now. Thurmond was holding the rope. Homer was shaking and scared and looking at the rope. Leroy said:

"Well, it's about that time."

They took hold of Homer and Homer said: "Come on, you guys. Now wait a minute. Oh, Jesus!"

Pierpont was sitting in the pickup. He was nervous but not as much as before. A. J. helped Homer into the seat and crawled in beside him. Everybody told Homer good-bye and then A. J. looked at Leroy.

"Where should we take him?"

Leroy said: "I don't know. Kansas City, maybe. Denver? Some place nice."

8

WHEN HOMER moved out, Superstition Pete moved in. Pete was a panhandler from Clarendon, Arkansas, who was sixty-eight years old, kept a talking parrot named Rose, a snaggle-toothed monkey by the name of Ringo, and drove a wagon with a wooden roof and foldaway sides pulled by a swayback, mangy horse he called Sonny.

Together, every year the four of them crossed and recrossed the country from the Mississippi Delta to the Rocky Mountains and were lately in from Laramie, Wyoming, with a fresh supply of arrowheads, rugs, and authentic Indian toothpaste made from pulverized pumice stone. He was bound for Jackson, Miss., and Mobile, Ala., and would spend the winter in Clarendon. He advertised his trade with two crescent-shaped signs on the foldaway sides that read:

SUPERSTITION PETE
Novelties and Gifts

He'd been traveling since the 1930s and Ringo was his second monkey. The first, Jess, had died at the age of fourteen, and Ringo was now going on twelve, and had lost some of his teeth as a casualty of age. But Rose, who was thirty-two, was his original parrot, and looked good for another five to ten years, for as everyone knows, parrots live a long time.

Pete had a chest-length beard and yellow teeth, like old piano keys, and his head was bald on top and as shiny as a button in the sun. He was short, his legs were stubby, and his eyes were sort of wild. His voice was shrill and he was apt to scream if he got too excited.

Pete had hit Berry City at a bad time. The people felt cheated by Homer's sudden and unannounced departure, and they had mean eyes for strangers. Pete had set up his wagon-store on the far side of the park and hadn't been there two days before some boys out cruising splattered Pete's wagon with eggs. It set Rose to squawking and almost scared Ringo to death. Mr. Manningham was still sore because Homer had run out on the twelfth day of a twenty-five-day contract and spoke to Mayor Sam about panhandlers, con artists, and chiselers. By the end of the week Sam had spoken to Police Chief Otis Taylor.

The day A. J. and Pierpont got back from Colorado, two cops on motorcycles were leading Pete and his wagon down Main Street toward the bridge. Pots, pans, chains, and lanterns jangled from the sides of the wagon, and the old wheels squeaked and squalled. Sonny was walking so slowly, the cops were having trouble with their cycles. The front wheels kept swiveling, and the cops had to brace with their legs and wait for Pete to catch up. It was a hot day, and the cops were sweating and losing patience. They kept telling Pete to hurry up.

Pete paid them no attention. He looked straight ahead and his eyes were dark and angry. Ringo was perched on the roof of the wagon, licking his fingers and looking, maybe a little nostalgically, at all the trees.

Pierpont was driving the pickup. He pulled around the wagon, and A. J. leaned out of the window and spoke to one of the cops.

"Where're you taking him?"

"Mind your own business, buddy. Move on."

Pierpont fanned himself with his hand and said: "I could use a beer."

"They ought not to treat the old geezer like that," A. J. said.

It was Friday afternoon—late—and Thurlo's place was jammed. Business as usual. When A. J. and Pierpont came in, Doodle had just finished a number, and Rainbow was going into her act. She walked around her table and in between two others and then stood perfectly for the applause. The boys whooped and yelled and beat on the tables with beer bottles while the girls sneered. A skinny boy in khaki pants and argyle socks got up and started for Rainbow with his arms outstretched. The guys at his table egged him on.

"That's it, Skeeter."

"Go on, man."

"Don't back down."

"Kiss her right, man."

Rainbow saw him coming and smiled. Jane Russell waiting for Henry Aldrich. She bumped herself into him and held it. Then she took his smooth face in her soft, warm hands and gave him a big, long smack. Skeeter's fingers clawed the air, and he went through the whole kiss with his eyes open. When it was over, he backed away trembling and sat down and quickly crossed his legs because there was a little tent in his pants.

Everybody roared.

Thurlo came over and shook A.J.'s hand. Then he shook Pierpont's. "Homer won't be back?" he asked A.J. "You're sure?"

"He won't be back."

Homer did turn up a couple of years later down in Chilpancingo, Mexico, where he set a Mexican record for flagpole sitting of forty-eight days that still stands. But he never came back to Arkansas.

Mae led A.J. and Pierpont out onto the deck followed by a waitress carrying a bucket of iced-down Falstaff. The beer was so cold the necks of the bottles were frosty. Mae said:

"If you need anything else, just holler. It's on the house."

A.J. and Pierpont pulled up chairs and raised their feet to the railing and settled back, prepared to watch the sunset. Inside, it sounded like a fire in a circus.

Across the river, which was outside the city limits and in the next county, Pete stopped his wagon on a pull-off and turned Sonny loose to graze along the bank. Then he started setting up shop. He climbed on top of the roof and he was carrying a shiny brass bell that had come off a steam locomotive. He fixed it to an upright and set Ringo down beside it and gave him the cord. The monkey knew exactly what to do and began ringing the bell like mad, hopping up and down and squealing as he yanked on the cord.

Next, Pete took down the sides of his wagon and lifted out

something covered with a sheet. He slipped off the sheet, revealing Rose, who began squawking immediately. The squawking was loud and carried even across the river.

People coming in and out of town stopped their cars and got out to see this monkey ringing the bell and to listen to Rose, who, as it turned out, had a vocabulary in English and Spanish. She was speaking Spanish that day and saying "Quiere coger? Quiere coger?" over and over again.

Inside the wagon on shelves Pete had jars, bottles, canisters, and boxes stacked up on several rows. They contained his arrowheads and Indian toothpaste as well as herbs, roots, spices, and seeds. On one end of the shelves were tricks and games and novelties like the dunking bird and false-bottom brandy snifters with liquid that wouldn't pour. Pete opened some boxes and brought rugs and articles of glass and pottery ware out to the side of the road and set them down. He had red and orange hooded cobras raised to strike, naked girls in gold, miniature deer, squirrels, and cats, and a couple of concrete birdbaths. Inside half an hour ten or twelve cars had stopped on the pull-off, and before sundown Pete had made $15.

He didn't stop there. After dark, Pete took four torches, doused them in kerosene, lit them and placed them in wire holders at the four corners of the wagon's roof. He gave Ringo a bowl of Wheaties and cream, and Ringo kept on ringing the bell even though it was night. But Pete put Rose to bed. When the sun was gone, he put on some flute music on his battery-powered victrola to go with the night. With the torches blazing, the bell ringing, and Ringo hopping around and the flute music, it all looked and sounded like some kind of early Egyptian sacrifice, and the cars kept on stopping. By nine o'clock, Pete had increased his take to $25.

Then he closed and went to bed, shutting himself up inside his wagon with the door locked and bolted and the sides also raised and latched with bent nails through hooks. Inside there, Pete was as secure as a mummy in a tomb. Pete had been robbed before.

Still, he woke up a poorer man.

The first thing Pete noticed the next morning was that Sonny was gone. Sonny wasn't much of a horse. Pete had picked him up from a rodeo rider in Amarillo, Texas, seven years ago for $60, and Sonny was a long way from his prime. Still, he was the only horse Pete had.

Pete cupped his hands to his mouth and called, but Sonny didn't come. Pete stomped down to the river, cursing and shaking his head, thinking Sonny might be getting himself a drink of water. If he had looked around the bend in the river on the other side of the bridge behind a clump of willows, it might have been a different story, but he didn't. He turned back and searched the fields and woods on the hill above the river. There was no sign of Sonny.

Then, it hit him. In his hurry to find the horse, he had left his wagon unguarded and the door unlocked. There was no one there but Ringo and a still sheeted Rose. Pete ran back toward the highway and his beard was swinging from side to side like a tail.

Son of a bitch!

Pete saw two guys wearing pilot helmets and goggles jump down from his wagon. One of them was carrying a steel box about the size of a pair of shoes that Pete kept his money in. The two guys disappeared below the cliff at the bridge, and when Pete got there, they were pushing off in a motorboat. It was a big boat without any number or name, and it had two twin 200-horsepower outboards on the stern that tore up the water like a whale. Sonny was standing in the back of the boat with his front legs braced to keep from falling. The boat and Sonny were out of sight in a matter of seconds.

About noon, Pete walked into Thurlo's with Ringo on a chain and Rose in her cage and started drinking beer. By one o'clock, Thurlo knew the whole story. He sent Mae out for some bananas for Ringo and gave Rose some popcorn. Then he called A. J. up at the Sands Motel. A. J. and Pierpont came right down.

Ringo was on his second banana and Rose was asleep in her cage under a bar towel. Pierpont sat down on the far side of the table away from Ringo with his hands in a guard position on his chest in case of a monkey attack.

"Put your money away if that's all you got left," A. J. told Pete. "You can drink on us. I'm getting an idea."

Pierpont said he thought it was about time they started back for DeValls, but he didn't press it.

Pete said: "I got people in Clarendon. But I can't get there with no horse. And I won't leave that wagon."

"Won't have to," A. J. said and took an Esso map out of his hip pocket. "This map's got rivers on it. Well, look, the Wassekia runs into the White about ten to fifteen miles north of DeValls, and judging from this, it's about twenty miles to the White. That's a trip of no more than thirty-five miles at the outside. We'll float you down to DeValls and you can make it on to Clarendon with no sweat."

"I don't know, Kid," Thurlo said. "Where'll you get a boat of a size to float his wagon?"

"It's heavy as hell," Pete said. "I don't want nothing to happen to my wagon."

"I'll be back in a couple of hours," A. J. said.

About three, A. J. pulled into the parking lot, and he was carrying six oil drums and some heavy lumber in the back of the pickup. The spouts at the top of the drums he had got welded at Drexel's Garage, and Drexel had said they would float like corks.

Everyone went to work with hammers and nails and rope and by seven that night, Pete's raft was built. They launched it during a break at Harroway's boat dock near the bridge and then brought Pete's wagon down to the water. They towed it with the pickup and the wagon squeaked and skirled and rattled and everybody thought it was going to break in two, but it didn't.

They rolled it out to the raft on boards and set it so the wheels were part way in the water. They had left a groove for the singletree between the drums, and it fit perfectly. The whole rig seemed sturdy enough, but to test it A. J. and Leroy got out on the pontoons and rocked it back and forth. It was OK, but to be sure, they put some sandbags on the four corners.

"OK, Rainbow," A. J. said. "Go ahead."

And Rainbow christened the raft with a bottle of Falstaff.

The bottle broke with a nice loud pop, and the beer foamed down the side of a drum. Everybody cheered.

They got an early start the next morning, just after day-break. Rose wasn't unsheeted yet and made no sound. Ringo was up on top of the roof with A. J. but he wasn't pulling on the bell cord. He looked a little scared of the water. Pete was in the bow with a pair of field glasses looking downriver. Pierpont stood on the stern with his suitcase looking like Paul Henreid in *Now Voyager*.

A. J. pushed off with an oar and poled the raft out into the current. It was pretty swift but flowing smoothly. He had made a rudder out of a chair seat and a six-foot two-by-four which he handled from the back of the roof.

The boys on the bank called out good-bye and good luck and Leroy said: "Let us know when you get there, and Will will drive your pickup down."

Rainbow and Mae were up on the bridge waving hand-kerchiefs. The sun was breaking over the haze in the east. It was a nice day for a boatride.

"We've come about ten miles I figure," A. J. said, looking at the Esso map when they pulled up to the gravel bar for the night. "Not bad for this old tub."

Pete started a fire on the gravel and began cooking some Campbell's pork and beans and frying hamburger. It smelled good, and Pierpont eyed the meat hungrily.

After supper, A. J. said it might be a good idea if they kept watch in case the robbers came back. Pierpont said he would take the first watch. Then A. J. said he would take over.

"Suits me," Pete said and went down into his wagon. He came up a minute later and he was carrying a shotgun. He patted it on the barrel and said: "Buckshot. I hope the sons of bitches do come back." Then he turned in.

They woke up the next morning in a light but steady rain. A. J. had been sleeping on the gravel bar and it drove him in-side the wagon. Pierpont was already awake. It was crowded in there with two men, Rose, and Ringo, and Ringo smelled terrible. Ringo was huddled in a corner licking his fingers and eyeing Pierpont with suspicion.

"I do not care for sleeping with a monkey," Pierpont said. "Or a parrot either, for that matter," he added and looked at Rose.

"Quiere coger?" Rose said to Pierpont and laughed.

Pete stuck his head inside and grabbed Ringo by the tail. Ringo went along with a little scream and after a moment they heard Ringo on the bell. Then Pete called out. "We're off."

The rain kept falling, harder. Thunder had been bickering off to the northwest, now it crackled directly over head. The wind came up and the rain swept across the river in sheets. The thunder boomed and the lightning split open the sky. Rose was squawking inside and Ringo was howling on the roof.

"This is a madhouse," Pierpont said and went outside even though it was raining buckets. He climbed up on the roof beside Ringo and started ringing the bell himself, angrily and defiantly, at nothing except the rain.

The rain began tapering off that afternoon, and A. J. steered the raft under a bridge at the little town of Dixon. They all got out and went up to the Crest Motel and had a shower and drank some beer while they were bathing and drying. After that, they went downtown and ate some fried chicken at a drive-in and walked back to the raft licking their fingers. They went to sleep right away and no one kept watch.

In the morning the skies had cleared. Pete found some dry wood under the bridge, and they had a breakfast of bacon and eggs and grits, which steamed on their tin plates like tiny white volcanoes. That tasted good and it was a better day already. A. J. said:

"We should make the White River by tomorrow. We ought to be home before the end of the week."

"None too soon," Pierpont said and poled the raft out into the current.

The river was getting wider now and the current wasn't as strong as the day they left. Still, they made pretty good time. They passed a lot of traffic that morning: the usual fishing boats and a couple of long barges owned by the Cardwell Company hauling cut lumber up and down the river. The company had another mill at Bledscoe downriver and A. J. was hoping to make it to Bledscoe that night.

They didn't quite.

The trouble started that afternoon at the little town of Weeds, two miles north of Bledscoe. A. J. looked back and noticed a large motorboat trailing them and gaining fast. It swung out to the left and came abreast of them about fifty yards away. A. J. could see the two 200-horsepower motors on the stern. There were two guys in the cabin and they were wearing pilot's helmets and goggles.

Pierpont was sitting outside with Rose trying to get her to say something in English, but she was still talking Spanish. Ringo was below taking a nap. Pete was scanning the river with his field glasses and then he saw the boat.

"It's them by shit!" he yelled and scampered below. He came back up with his shotgun and he was firing almost before he got outside. He used up his shells and went below to reload.

The motorboat turned and headed for the raft at top speed. When it was a short distance away, one of the guys in helmets swerved. The motorboat shot across the bow, and great rolling waves smacked into the side of the wagon-raft. It rocked like a bassinet, and water splashed over the drums and into the wagon and streamed out the other side.

Rose was swept overboard and died screaming in Spanish. Pete was still inside the wagon, rolling around and clawing for balance. Jars and boxes tumbled off the shelves, and the floor of the wagon was littered with broken hooded cobras and busted glass squirrels and golden girls snapped in half. Up ahead, a barge loaded with lumber was coming upstream under a railroad bridge.

The motorboat turned for another pass, this time heading in at an angle toward the bow. The driver swerved again at the last moment and the waves slammed into the raft. The drums on the port side came clear out of the water before they righted again. Pierpont was up front holding on and was of no use to anyone. Pete was still trying to get up below.

A. J. kept sculling with the rudder and trying to maneuver

the raft in close behind the protection of the barge. The guys in the motorboat could see what he was doing and they turned and came in again at full speed. But the driver swerved too late this time and the motorboat swiped one of the drums and headed out into the middle of the river, zigzagging crazily.

The collision had probably sheered one or both of the control cables, because a few seconds later the two guys jumped off the speeding boat and they were still wearing their helmets and goggles.

Then came the crash. The man in the wheelhouse on the lumber barge saw it coming. He ran outside screaming and climbed up on the stacks of lumber waiting for the impact. The motorboat rammed straight into the barge at full speed and skewered the wheelhouse like a hotdog. The barge began to swing around out of control and headed back downstream toward the railroad bridge. Then fire broke out on the barge.

The barge was going about five miles an hour when it struck the timbers in the bridge, but the barge weighed nearly fifty tons with all that lumber. The timbers of the bridge buckled and cracked and ties fell down into the water. The sailors on the barge jumped overboard, and on the far shore, A. J. could see the guys in helmets running up the bank.

The fire spread fast across the lumber. The flames crept up into the bridge, and smoke rose in great black columns into the warm, sunny afternoon sky.

Pete finally made it back up top, and when he saw the fire he started jumping up and down and shaking his gun. His eyes were wild. Then he started looking around for Rose. "Rose?" he cried. "Rose!"

A. J. eased the raft around the barge, keeping close to the bank, and Pierpont poled with the oar. They were about a hundred feet below the bridge when the tanks on the barge went up, and that was the final end to the bridge. It was crackling with flames. The rails dangled over the water and the barge grunted with little explosions before it sank.

"God damn," A. J. said softly.

What was gone was a railroad bridge, a barge, a load of lumber, a motorboat, and a parrot. The papers said a few days later the total loss came to over half a million dollars.

A. J. cracked a beer and looked thoughtfully at the ruins. He was thinking about Joe and how Joe would take the news. He was still considering that when a red-hot rail came loose from the tracks and fell hissing into the water.

A. J. leaned back against the side of the wagon and closed his eyes.

"Well, God damn," he said again, even more softly.

Pete got himself a beer and took out his field glasses, searching in vain for Rose. Pierpont sat disconsolately in the bow, not drinking. Smoke was still boiling up from the bridge, and it spread out in a long, wide trail across the sky. Sirens were going everywhere. Horns were honking and there was a train whistle way off in the distance.

Ringo sat up on the roof by the bell. After a moment, he started pulling the cord. He rang the bell softly, almost tolling it, as if he knew.

9

THEY PULLED into A. J.'s boat dock on Friday and Alvin came down to meet them.

"There's a guy named Apple here looking for you, Kid. Says you knew him at Tucker and promised him a job. Also, your aunt up in Batesville called. Said it was urgent. Where'd you get that rig? Jesus Christ! Look at that monkey!"

"It's a long story," A. J. said and turned to Pete. They shook hands and Pete said:

"I'll pay you back for them pontoons and lumber when I get the money."

"Forget it. See you around, Pete."

Pete shook his hand again and shoved off for Clarendon.

"Who was that?" Alvin asked when they were walking up to the house.

"Friend of ours. Got robbed by a couple of river rats. Tried to swamp us on the way down. You say Doris called?"

"Yeah. Say, did you hear about the mess up near Bledscoe? Lumber barge hit a railroad bridge and everything caught fire."

"Yeah we did."

Larry Apple was waiting for them at the house.

"Hey, old buddy," A. J. said. "How's it going?"

"Got out last week, Kid. I remembered what you said."

"Still goes. We'll talk about it. But can you wait a minute? I got a phone call to make."

A few minutes later, A. J. came back from the phone. "Look," he told Larry. "I got to leave town. You can start today. Pierpont here will show you around. He's an expert." Then to Pierpont he said:

"Joe's missing. I need to borrow your car."

"Sure, Kid. Anything you want. Take care."

On Wednesday, Joe Lynly had read in the paper about the big trestle fire north of Bledscoe and had gone up into his tower. On Thursday he had put on his conductor's uniform and walked downtown to Bea Coulter's bakery and told Bea: "You won't have to worry about shipping your pies and cakes today, Mrs. Coulter. The trains aren't running."

Next, Joe had stepped into Laggett's drugstore and warned Elmo Woodson, the soda jerk, to keep his stainless steel shining and the bar and the clubcar swept clean even though the trains were stopped. "Don't let up on the job," Joe told him. "That's no way to run a railroad."

The word passed around: Joe was having another spell, and everyone who saw Joe that day downtown played along. When he got to Vic Singleton's Hardware down by the bridge, Vic was wearing his engineer's cap, and he acted worried.

"What's the news?" Joe asked.

Vic told him of hot boxes and broken tracks. Trains were running late all over the system, he said, and the 210 from Kansas City was creeping toward Little Rock with two units out. Joe nodded his head. Vic went on: There were strikes and wrecks and the government had threatened to move in. Joe nodded again and said:

"Something has got to be done this time. I've waited too long."

Vic patted Joe on the shoulder. "Don't worry now. It's out of our hands. Things will get better tomorrow. You'll see."

Vic's wife Alice helped him out in the store. When Joe left, she said: "You ought not to play along like that. I don't like it."

"Well, you can't blame me," Vic said angrily and went back to work.

That night, after supper, Joe climbed slowly up to his room in the attic. He came down an hour later and he was still dressed. His old black uniform was slick and shiny with wear, but he had polished his brass buttons, and his shoes shone like obsidian. He carried his black leather traveling bag. He walked past Doris without a word and into the kitchen. There, he reached into the cupboard and took down some tin cans and a bottle of whiskey and placed them in his bag.

"I'm going on a trip," he told Doris. "Can't tell when I'll get back."

Doris hardly knew what to say. Her mouth turned down and her eyes were hollow with dismay. She was frozen in her seat. Joe leaned down and kissed her good-bye and then he turned and walked proudly from the room and down the front porch steps.

That's when Doris had made her call to A. J.

A. J. looked at Doris. "You didn't tell the cops?"

"I couldn't. I just can't. I'm afraid they'll lock him up. There have been hints."

"Well, you settle down, now. We'll find Joe. Do you know where he was going? Which way he was headed?"

Doris was trying not to cry. "He stopped by Jory's drive-in last night. Jory called to tell me. Said Joe had asked him if the 210 was in yet from Kansas City. All Jory said was he was walking west. Went off into the woods, talking about seeing the president of the railroad. Oh, you've just got to find him!"

A. J. followed Joe four days through the mountains and the woods. He found his tracks and his fires and patches of his coat torn away on bushes and thorns. And he talked to people who had seen him.

"Sure. He was here," a man told him in Melbourne, thirty miles away. "Didn't know that was his name. Kept asking if the train was on time. There ain't no train through here. He was as crazy as a coot."

The White River ferryman at Sylamore remembered him. "Yep. He rode over yesterday morning. Kept saying how much smaller the Mississippi was than it used to be. He thought this was the Mississippi River, mister." The ferryman shook his head. "I didn't charge to take him across since he was walking. He headed up through the hills there to Fifty-Six. Didn't take the road, though, so I can't say for sure."

"Thanks."

"Funny thing though."

"Yeah?"

"He kept saying how bad the trains were. That there was wrecks everywhere and nobody could stop them. And did you know there was one this morning up near Cotter? Twelve cars derailed on a fast freight, the radio said. Second time this year. And I guess you heard the trestle's out over by Bledscoe. You know, he's right. Somebody ought to do something."

"Yeah. Well, thanks again."

The next morning A. J. talked to a man in Fifty-Six.

"You looking for him?" the man said. "Why? You the police?"

A. J. shook his head.

"Maybe you're from one of them mental hospitals. It wouldn't surprise me none."

"No. He's a friend of mine. A relative in fact. He's lost."

The man thought about that for a moment then said: "Well, last I seen of him he was headed back that way." He pointed over the mountains in the direction of the river. "Toward Sylamore. He looked pretty beat. Said he hadn't ate lately. Looked it. Offered him a sandwich, but he couldn't stop. Said he had to see the president of the railroad. Didn't say which one, but it don't matter. There ain't one up here."

A. J. found him that night on a mountain that overlooked the White River Valley. The moon was full and straight overhead. The wind was strong out of the west and the trees whooshed and snapped, and their branches played furious games of tag with their shadows on the ground.

Joe was standing in a little clearing. He looked bad. His uniform was ripped and torn, and tatters hung down from his conductor's cap. His shoes were dirty and heelless, his black bag was scratched and one of the handles had come off. The clearing was cluttered with rocks and old stumps, and high grasses grew around the rocks and the stumps. In the center of the clearing was an old watchtower that was now tumbled down, its beams crossed and broken grotesquely. To the right of this and at the edge of the clearing was a tall, full maple tree. Beyond, down in the valley, lights along the river twinkled like stars.

Joe had made a fire of leaves and sticks. The wood was flaming and the yellow lights were flickering on Joe's face and making his shadow dance behind him on the trees. Joe opened his bag and took out what was left of the bottle of whiskey. He raised the bottle, and the whiskey was warm in his cheeks and raw in his throat. He was about to address the fallen tower when A. J. stepped into the clearing.

"Hello, Joe," A. J. said softly.

Joe looked at him with narrow eyes. "Well, you kept me waiting!" he said fiercely. "Sit down there and listen to me!"

"All right, Joe."

A. J. sat down on a rock. Joe sat facing him on a stump across the clearing. He took another drink from the bottle and said:

"I was sent here. Never mind by who. You've had your time, now you must get ready to take your medicine." He raised his voice ferociously. "You get ready. YOU HEAR?"

The wind died down suddenly, and it was very quiet on the mountain. The fire crackled softly and the maple tree barely moved. It seemed to lean down to listen.

"Yes, sir, Joe."

"That's better." Joe leaned forward. He crooked his finger at A. J. savagely. "I know you, Jacob Travis. You're the president of this mighty railroad and your father was president of it before that and your granddaddy laid track. But that don't matter now. No, sir, it don't count. You're in deep trouble and the road is going to ruin and now the time is here."

Joe nodded his head vigorously in support of his statement, and then he shouted: "Sit still there. I'm not through with you yet!" Joe drank again quickly and put the bottle down.

"Who sent me? you want to know." Joe laughed in scorn. "No, you wouldn't know. Well, it was all of them. The dead and gone. The good men who done the work, good work, and were replaced by worser men. And all of them people out there who rode the line. The ones you never cared about, because you said people don't count. Just profits!"

Joe's eyes were white with fury and his fists were clenched as he finished this. Then his eyes softened, his voice fell low and he looked out over the valley. "I'm telling them, Doris. I'm telling them the way it is, and they don't like it." His voice climbed upward and out of the clearing into the night sky. "YOU GOD DAMN RIGHT THEY DON'T!"

The wind came up again and there was a rustling in the maple tree and its top branches swirled. Joe raised the bottle high and drank with great satisfaction. He looked at A. J., facing him squarely.

"You, sir, Mr. Jacob Travis, are stepping down. That's right." His eyes swept from the broken tower beams across the stumps and rocks in the clearing to the maple tree. "All of you! You're through. As sure as the stars turn, you've had it!"

Joe looked at them with his chin thrust forward. He could see them very clearly now, their round faces with eyeglasses and their fingers shining with rings. Joe rose to his feet.

"They have sent me, and I have the money." He reached down for his black bag, opened it and checked inside. And then he snapped it shut. "We're buying you out and you are fired for good. Once and for all!" He hurled the bag across the clearing. It rolled over the rocks and came to rest on its side. "Take the money. Take your profits and run. We're going to save the railroad! And it's going to be a GREAT RAILROAD! JUST LIKE IT USED TO BE!"

Joe raised his arms. He looked around, as if to a throng, and in the maple tree the wind moved the leaves. Joe picked up the bottle and finished it and then he threw it against the rocks. It broke with a loud pop. It was very quiet.

A. J. stood up. "We'll be going now, Joe," A. J. said. "Like you say."

Joe sat back down. "Yeah," he said. "You damn right you will." His eyes were hot and his vision was blurry. But slowly he saw the beams of the tower begin to move. And the stumps and the rocks moved with them. They rolled and jostled each other silently and then they floated away, tumbling into the darkness until they were gone.

A. J. held out his hand. "Come on, Joe. Let's go home."

Joe got up and looked intently into A. J.'s eyes. Then he smiled. "Hey, it's you, Kid, ain't it? Well, we did it. Yes, sir, we did it this time, didn't we, Kid?"

"You bet, Joe."

They caught a ride with a guy in a ton and a half who was going to Batesville. Joe got in the cab between them and his head sagged on his chest. He was tired. The guy in the truck noticed this but said nothing for a couple of miles. Finally, when Joe looked like he was asleep, the man said: "What happened to him? He looks bad. There been another train wreck around here some place?"

Joe rose part way out of his seat and his eyes were kind of wild. A. J. had to take hold of him and force him back. "Take it easy, Joe. You're the new president of the railroad. Everything's OK."

The guy behind the wheel looked queerly at A. J. He was going to say something, but A. J. told him:

"Just keep driving."

It was midnight when they got to Batesville.

Doris saw them coming up the front porch. She opened her arms in joy and ran out to meet them. She hugged Joe and held him and helped him up the steps. At the top of the steps, Joe took hold of her by the shoulders. He looked down at her and stood tall with dignity and pride and said:

"We have just bought the railroad. Everything will be all right now. We've come through. It's over. I'll tell Vic first thing in the morning. Everything is going to be all right."

Doris looked at A. J., and her eyes were misty and shining. "Oh, thank God," she murmured and buried her face in Joe's coat. "Oh, thank God!"

10

THE BAND had been on a little vacation in Hot Springs where they'd lain around in the baths and taken in the sights, which always meant watching a chicken named Joe DiMaggio play baseball at the I.Q. Zoo and going by for feeding time at the Alligator Farm. Leroy and his crew and A. J. and Pierpont were coming into Forrest City about dinnertime, and Leroy was grumbling because he wanted a steak like he'd had at Jud's a couple of nights ago.

"I'd sure like one of them New York strips," Leroy said. "But you can't get a good piece of meat in this part of the country. They're as scarce as niggers in Montana."

Rainbow had been reading *Silver Screen*, and she looked up from her magazine.

"What do you know about Montana?" she said, for it was a known fact she'd argue with Leroy about anything.

"I was through there once on the train. It was during Korea."

"On the train?" Rainbow said and laughed.

"You can tell a lot about the country on the train."

"And you didn't see no niggers from your parlor car, so there ain't none. Is that right?"

"Yeah. That's right."

"I bet I could find one."

"No you couldn't."

"Yeah I could, too!"

Rainbow was getting kind of hot, and Will said from the back seat: "I wish you was both in Montana." That ended the argument.

They stopped at Deena's Cafe, and Leroy ordered a bowl of chili instead of a steak. He said Deena's steaks were as hard to cut as license plates. But he didn't say it around Deena. She was pretty tough.

Deena brought him a bowl of chili, and Leroy was eating it but not liking it very much.

Rainbow was still reading *Silver Screen*, and she'd come across a story about a girl named Stella Turner from Bossier Parish, Louisiana, who'd been a beauty queen in high school before she'd got a part with Stewart Granger in *King Solomon's Mines*.

Rainbow looked at Leroy and said: "I wanna be a beauty queen!"

"This shit tastes like that Lax-Tex you get down in Dallas," Leroy said about the chili.

"How's that?" Deena said from over by the service window.

"Nothing," Leroy said. "Just that I'd like a steak."

"I got steaks," Deena said, her eyes narrowing.

"Naw, this is all right," Leroy said, and Deena let it go.

"Did you HEAR me?" Rainbow said.

She had to lean down to get his attention because Leroy always ate chili and soup with his face close to the bowl. The chili was hot with fire. Little beads of sweat had formed on his brow from the rising steam and the back of his collar was wet. He slurped once and kept spooning. His tongue was already stinging.

"What do you think, Kid?" Leroy said.

A. J. looked thoughtful but for the moment said nothing. He was sitting in a booth with Pierpont. Will, Thurmond, and Pepper were stationed on stools at the counter like owls on a branch drinking bottles of beer and eating hamburgers. Rainbow and Leroy were just a little way down the counter from them. Deena was at the register now, scowling at Doodle Socket because he was taking up a whole booth by himself.

That was something new with Doodle Socket. He had announced a couple of weeks before that from then on he would eat alone. He'd got that from Bobby Joe Sadler. Bobby Joe was one of the best country singers around at that time. Well, he had come into the Peabody Hotel dining room in Memphis one day wearing dark glasses and accompanied by two or three boys in shiny suits and a curvy, long-legged redhead in satin pants. What had surprised Doodle was that Bobby Joe sat at a corner table all by himself. Everybody else was looking at him, including Doodle Socket, who picked up the trick right away as a means of letting people know who was the star. From then on he had started wearing dark glasses all the time. He was wearing them now, but he slipped them off every once in a while so he could be recognized.

Doodle, of course, still drove alone. He had recently bought a brand new 1956 T-Bird, painted a bright, banana yellow, and this one didn't have the Captain Marvel streak down the side. Doodle had had it up to 125, and it ran, as he said, as smooth as a calf sucking. But it was in the shop now. Doodle had found a fast stretch over near Stuttgart a week before and had rolled it twice before it ended up with its wheels spinning in a borrow ditch. Doodle had come out of it all right, but his new T-Bird was a mess. He was now forced to ride in company, but he ate by himself.

Rainbow was waiting for an answer and she was getting tired of waiting.

A. J. said: "What makes you think you can be a beauty queen?"

"Ha!" Rainbow said. She swung around a couple of times on her stool, looking A. J. and the others over and letting her dress fly up over her thighs. She wrapped her legs together like climbing snakes and leaned her elbows back on the counter and threw out her chest. Leroy's face came up from his chili, and the three owls at the counter swung their heads to watch this. A man in a booth started choking on some potato chips, and his little girl had to pound his back.

A man and his wife came in and took the last open booth. Deena wrote down their order and breezed by Doodle Socket. Then on second thought she stopped, turned back to Doodle Socket and called out the order. "Gimme one special. Hold the peas. One burger." She was looking straight at Doodle Socket. "NO SMELL!" She glared at him for a moment then turned on a dime and went back to her register. Doodle Socket took off his glasses and smiled.

Rainbow kept drumming her fingernails on the counter. "Well," she said to Leroy. "What do you say?"

"The one thing I can't ever figure out is how come the beans are always hottern the chili," Leroy said. He curled his tongue and sucked in a stream of cool air.

Rainbow was furious. She came down hard on the counter with her knuckles. "I want to be a beauty queen!"

"Rainbow," he said, "that might take some time. More than we got. You need money, too."

"We're in between dates," she said. "What have we got on so hot this summer?"

Leroy lowered his voice slightly. "Anyhow, we're married. Well, not exactly, but we sort of are under that common law."

"It's common all right!" Rainbow snapped.

Leroy was unruffled. "Trouble with women is you're never satisfied. You want this, you want that. If I was to give in on this, next time you'd be asking for the moon."

Rainbow leaned over to him again and smiled, a little too nicely. "Sweetie," she said, "fuck the moon. I wanna be a beauty queen."

Leroy ordered a beer and looked over at A. J. A. J. was staying out of it. Leroy tried to be reasonable. "Look, Rainbow, you and me, we got kids. Now where'd you ever hear of a beauty queen with kids?" Deena brought Leroy his beer.

Rainbow scowled. Leroy was using the kids against her and that was mean. She swung around on her stool again and kicked at some imaginary thing in the air, and then her right eye started to roll. Leroy saw it and looked away. He didn't like it, and he was afraid of it. The man in the booth saw it too and said something to his wife, but she didn't turn around.

Will said: "Aw, it's probably happened lots of times before, only nobody mentioned it."

"Yeah," Rainbow said. "Who's gonna know? There's money in it besides. Remember me telling you about Bitsy Shillcut from Carlisle?"

Leroy said no.

"Oh, yes you do! She wasn't nothing really. Pretty hair, but skinny. She could slide through a drainpipe. But she made it to one of them big-time beauty pageants and come away with a brand new T-Bird just like Doodle's. She got her start as a poultry princess from Lonoke County."

"A chicken queen," Leroy said with a sneer.

That seemed to squelch it and nobody said a word. But after a moment, A. J. got up and came over to Rainbow. He put his hands under her chin and tilted it this way and that and said:

"I don't know, boys. It might be that this here is a super chick."

Rainbow let out a squeal of joy. She gave A. J. a kiss and reached over for Leroy's beer. She took it right out of his hands, eyed him defiantly and drank a great long drink.

Leroy dropped his head into his hands. "God all mighty," he said.

Molly Fitlowe was Flossie's sister. Molly ran the Shake Loose Club in Marked Tree, and the boys stopped by to see her because once upon a time Molly had been a beauty queen.

"You wouldn't know it to look at her," Doodle Socket said acidly from the back seat of Leroy's car and glared at everybody.

Leroy was driving. Rainbow was sleeping with her head against his shoulder and with a smile on her face. She was dreaming about the Cadillacs and furs she was going to win as a big-time beauty queen. The others were in the back with Doodle Socket. Will was yodeling quietly. Thurmond was eating a ham sandwich which he had chewed down to one small square he could barely hold in his fingers, and he was taking tiny bites to keep from finishing it. Pepper's eyes were trying to control the bouncing letters in his book on pharmacology and he was worrying about his acne. He gave his eyes a rest and looked at his reflection in the window. His acne was no better, and he turned away with a frown. The hot peppers hadn't helped. He'd spent a lot of money on salves and lotions and $6 for one of Dr. Brinkley's pimple ejectors, but nothing worked. Maybe one day, when he owned that drugstore.

Doodle Socket kept scowling at Thurmond, wishing he'd finish that sandwich. He felt crowded and pinched in the back with the others and saw no reason why Rainbow should hog the front seat. A. J. and Pierpont had gone ahead, and they hadn't offered him a ride. Doodle Socket missed his car and that bothered him the most. His love life was impaired without wheels, and he had no confidence in himself with girls. It would be a week before Luther Slight would have it ready over in Stuttgart. Meantime, Doodle was a passenger, and he didn't like it.

"Piss!" he said and lapsed into silence, his mind swarming with terrible scenes of bloody revenge and secret assassinations. Nobody paid any attention to him. At such times it was better to leave Doodle Socket alone.

But Doodle was right about Molly. She was nothing to look at any more. Her hair was stringy and she was forty; she was fat on beer and her two front teeth had been broken in a brawl. But she still had great legs, she could drink and dance all night, and she was a realist. The first thing she said when A. J. told her about Rainbow was that it was a tough business and that you had to be smart.

Then she cracked some beers and they all went into her office to have a conference. The boys pulled up chairs around Molly's desk, but Doodle Socket sat in a corner looking out at a flooded rice field. Occasionally, he glanced over at Rainbow with thickening irritation. Rainbow was sitting on the edge of Molly's desk with her legs crossed already acting like a beauty queen. Every once in a while she would jerk into a little pose and smile.

The only other person there was Molly's bouncer, Shade Slade. They had been together for a long time, ever since the day over in Memphis when Shade had come into the Peabody Hotel lobby with his girl, Maud, to show her the ducks in the Peabody fountain. Molly was staying at the hotel at the time.

There is quite a ceremony involved with these ducks and every afternoon at four o'clock to the accompaniment of music they are led across a red carpet and into an elevator carrying them to their roost on the roof. That day Shade and his girl got there too late and missed the ceremony. Shade got mad.

He told Maud to wait and went up on the roof. He grabbed one of the ducks by the neck and brought him back down to the lobby. He set the creature down at the fountain and said:

"All right, duck, you walk!"

Molly had been impressed. Not just by Shade's quickness to act but by the fact that he whipped four elevator men, a house detective, the duckmaster, and the headwaiter from the Skyway during the episode.

Shade went just about everywhere with Molly now, but he seldom said a word. His remark to the duck is supposed to have been his longest utterance on anything. You knew he was the bouncer because he had a cauliflower ear and was scarred like a workbench. (He had once been a pretty good professional fighter.) And he wore steel-tipped cowboy boots. He was also the best starer in Poinsett County. He kept the peace at Molly's by staring at people when they were about to get out of line, and since nobody was able to look at Shade for very long, they minded their own business.

Molly said: "I'll tell you this, you got to have a sponsor."

"What's that mean?" Leroy said.

"I mean these beauty pageants can run into big money. You got to have pictures made and you need a wardrobe. That kind of stuff. I knew a girl once who was a poultry princess from Bald Knob. Forget her name. But she had a gang of sponsors. Hardware and feed stores, the Chamber of Commerce, and a horse doctor. Just about everybody. Needed them all, too, 'cause that girl ran up a hell of a bill. Heard it was close to a thousand dollars."

Rainbow grinned.

"Well, she went on to be a queen, but that's something else you got to watch out for. It wadn't worth it. She won all right, but all they gave her as a prize was a crate of eggs and a trip to Memphis to see the Travelers play the Memphis Chicks. I mean it. That's all she got. There are risks in this business and you can believe me."

Leroy frowned and looked at A. J. "Didn't think of that."

"I'm worth it," Rainbow said and struck a pose.

Molly said: "Why don't you try this. Go see the other road-house operators, Billy Luke and Blackie, and Flossie. I'll help you. Maybe you can scare up three-four hundred dollars. Course, you wouldn't want our names mentioned." Molly hunched over her desk and her eyes glowed like red-hot pokers. "But wouldn't it be a kick if she won something with people like us for sponsors?" Molly threw back her head and bared her teeth and roared. "Wouldn't that be a kick?"

Shade smiled and went out to the bar and brought everybody a beer.

A. J. had been thinking. "I was reading in the paper the other day about this reformation league down in Texas . . ." His voice trailed off and he was looking directly at Molly. There was a gleam in his eye and an answering one in hers. If you could have electrified them, they would have met in the middle of the room with a tiny explosion.

Molly laughed and stood up. "That's it. Rainbow's going into the beauty business and she's going to be sponsored in style. We'll call ourselves 'The Central Arkansas Reformation League.'"

That hit everybody just right. Even Shade smiled again. But Doodle Socket said:

"She don't look like no reform leaguer to me."

Rainbow whipped around on top of the desk. She moved fast and snaky and swung her left leg and let fly at him with her high-heeled shoe. Doodle Socket ducked with a little scream, and the shoe went past him and through the glass window onto the gravel parking lot.

Doodle jumped up. "Watch out, Rainbow. You can hurt somebody with a thing like that!" Rainbow just grinned. Shade went outside to the lot to get Rainbow's shoe. He didn't say a word.

Leroy came over and eased Rainbow off the desk. She was a little lopsided in one stocking foot. Leroy said: "You think you can look like a reformer, gal?"

Rainbow rubbed up against him and purred. "Reform who?"

A. J. and Leroy split up the next morning to find contributors to Rainbow's cause. Thurmond rode with A. J. and Pierpont, and Leroy took the rest. Doodle Socket stayed at Molly's and called Luther Slight over in Stuttgart every morning to see how Luther was coming on the car. Luther said: "It takes time, son. I can't fix 'em as fast as you can wreck 'em."

A. J. stopped first to see Billy Luke Short who owned the Red Eye over in Trumann and Billy Luke gave them $25. Then they drove up to see Chester at the Blue Swan. They stayed a few days with Chester, and Chester gave them $50. On the way back, they stopped by O'Brien Davis' Officers' Club in Blytheville and then saw Blackie Traynor at the Buckshot in West Memphis. They got $25 both places.

After that they swung by Brinkley and DeValls and paid a call on Pete and Maggie Dennison, who owned the Delta Ace and then on Jim Bob. Pete and Maggie gave them $35 but Jim Bob could only spare $5. Jim Bob was a good old boy but he was kind of tight.

They all met back at Molly's and counted the take. Leroy had seen Flossie, Duke Sikes in Forrest City, Percy Simms in Helena, and Stoplight Riley just outside of Marianna, and a few others. Leroy laid $100 on Molly's desk. All together, they had $265. That's when Pierpont said:

"I have a little something to contribute." He reached into his billfold and placed two crisp $50 bills on the desk. "There," he said and stepped back from the money. He looked uncomfortable.

"Well, Jesus!" Leroy said.

A. J. pumped his hand. "That's a lot of money, Pierpont."

Rainbow gave him a kiss and the others crowded around him and slapped him on the back.

Pierpont said: "I am a little surprised myself. I saved it when I was working for the Kid when he was on the farm. I know I will never see that money again. Indeed, it may help cause some terrible kind of disaster. You all know me. My feelings of caution and perspicacity are well known." He paused a moment. "However, I would like for this enterprise to succeed, and I am going to help out in this modest way."

"That's a damn fine thing to do," Will said quietly.

"You bet your ass it is!" Pepper said and picked up one of the fifties. He'd never handled a $50 bill.

Leroy grinned. "We got over three hundred dollars there."

"More than that," Molly said and reached into a cash box in a drawer. She took out a $100 bill and added it to the stack. "You forgot about me."

Shade Slade was next. He stepped forward and laid $5 in ones on the pile. Then he backed up without a word.

"You're nice too," Rainbow told him, "even though you don't say nothing most of the time." And she gave him a close, hard hug. Shade came up on the toes of his steel-tipped boots. His hands were behind his back and his head was raised and his eyes rolled like he was being hanged. When Rainbow was through, she ran her hands down Shade's chest, and a little shiver passed through Shade's body.

That made $470. After that, everyone dug into their pockets and chipped in what they had. It came to $493.12.

"We've got nearly half a grand," Leroy said and looked around for Doodle Socket just as the door closed and Doodle slipped out. Well, his car was in the shop and you couldn't get a brand new T-Bird fixed for nothing.

The next day, they dropped by Stuttgart to pick up Doodle Socket's car. It was ready and parked outside Luther's garage. The bill under the wiper said $149.50.

"Jesus Christ!" Doodle said and went inside. Luther was lying on the creeper under a pickup and the radio was on. Doodle bent down and slapped the bill. "This comes to a hundred and forty-nine dollars and fifty god damn cents!"

"Just a minute, son," Luther said. "I'll be right with you."

"And I ain't had my car the better part of three weeks," Doodle Socket yelled over the sound of the music. A. J. and Leroy came over, and Doodle Socket showed them the bill.

Luther got up wiping his hands with a rag and said: "I don't do rush jobs. I take my time and do it right, and with me time is money." That's when he saw Rainbow.

She was standing by the side of the car, and she yelled over to Leroy and A. J.

"Don't you go give him any of that money for the contest. Let the stingy bastard foot his own bill!"

"Who is that?" Luther breathed.

They told him she was Rainbow Wimberly from Hazen and that she was going to be the state's number one beauty queen.

"Get's my vote," Luther said, and then he looked at Doodle Socket and offered him a deal. Doodle Socket could take the car for $100 flat if Luther could have just one dance with Rainbow.

"Sure," Doodle Socket said, but Leroy said wait a minute. Rainbow was wearing a new dress they had bought for her that morning in Forrest City, a cool-looking yellow chiffon number that had cost $27.50. And Luther was not all that clean coming off the creeper.

A. J. and Leroy talked it over with Rainbow and Rainbow said: "I ain't fixing to two-step with a grease monkey for nobody." But when Luther promised to get clean, she said she'd think about it. "But you won't use none of that contest money to pay his bill?"

"Nope."

So they all stood around and waited while Luther went around back to wash. A few minutes later, Luther emerged from the washroom with his hair combed, wearing a fresh white shirt, clean pants, and smelling of Lava soap, and Rainbow said:

"Aw, what the hell."

Eddie Arnold was singing "Anytime" on the radio in the pickup. Rainbow put her arms around Luther and they danced to "Anytime" and right through a Riceland Foods commercial and to the end of the next number. Their feet moved lightly on the sawdust and they twirled under the engine hoist. It was beautiful. Rainbow said later Luther was a pretty good dancer.

Gratitude was a thing still-born in Doodle Socket and doomed as a trait, but it struck him now with a strange and sudden force. He owed Rainbow something. There was no way around it. But he handled it badly. He muttered his thanks awkwardly, and it sounded almost as if he was angry. Rainbow just told him to forget it.

But later on that afternoon, Doodle came by the Pastime where A. J. and the others were trying to decide which beauty contest Rainbow ought to enter first and Doodle was carrying a white box with a blue ribbon around it. In the box was a pink and purple orchid he had bought for a dollar and a half. Everyone was surprised, Rainbow most of all, and she got up and gave Doodle Socket a nice kiss. It happened right there in the middle of the smoke-filled room with twenty guys playing dominoes, and a feeling of richness and warmth came over everybody.

That night A. J. was reading the Stuttgart *Daily Leader* in the lobby of the Riceland Hotel, and on the front page was a story about two fishing derbys over in Clarendon. It seems that in the beginning there was to have been just one fishing derby for the most bass caught and one girl who would be crowned Miss Bass. Well, that had made the crappie fishermen mad and they had decided to hold their own derby and crown their own queen.

Both events were preliminaries to the White River Water Carnival and Beauty Pageant that was to be held in Batesville August 12–16. Miss Bass would receive a brand new rod and reel worth $45 plus some baits, and Miss Crappie would get an eight-foot fiber glass boat. Neither prize was all that much, but whoever went on to be the White River Carnival queen would come away with a $1,000 cash prize and a $1,500 mink coat. That was a booty worth having. The Miss Bass entries were closed, but the Miss Crappie people, since they had started late, were still looking for potential queens. The contest was to be held at the end of the week, and it was only Tuesday.

That's where Rainbow ought to start, A. J. said, and Leroy agreed, although he had been leaning toward the Timber Queen Pageant down in Crossett.

The next morning at breakfast, Doodle Socket had recovered from his attack of gratitude and announced he was driving to Memphis to see his agent Trent Dangerfield, who was still working to get him on the Ed Sullivan Show. It was just a matter of time, Doodle said, when they would get tired of that fucking Elvis. Trent also knew a lot of people in Hollywood, and Doodle said he might have to go out there and talk to some producers.

"Maybe I'll see you in Batesville," he said, "unless I'm out there making screen tests."

"Good-bye, Doodle Socket. Stay loose."

A. J. and Pierpont went up to DeValls for a couple of days to check in with Alvin and Larry Apple and said they would come down to Clarendon Wednesday night or Thursday. Leroy and the others drove on to Clarendon to get ready. On the way, it occurred to Will that Rainbow might be recognized as a professional nightclub performer. It was Will's thinking that with the wonders people could work with makeup and if Rainbow wouldn't mind dyeing her hair, the risks could be minimized.

Rainbow set him straight in a hurry. "Nobody's gonna dye my hair. Forget it. I ain't never had a thing on my gorgeous blonde hair and I ain't fixing to start now."

Leroy looked at her sharply, but Will said: "Let me talk."

"Look, Rainbow, sometimes in the interests of what's best for all, people have got to make sacrifices. Now, wait a minute. Hear me out. Did you know that hardly a one of them Hollywood actresses has their own hair color? That's no lie. And some of them even get their faces changed permanent, and when they're up there on that big, color screen, their own kinfolks don't even know who they are. They're still beautiful, but don't look like the original thing at all. That's how you get to be a star."

The word "star" did it. "Well, maybe," Rainbow said, "about dyeing my hair."

Will went on. "And we'll dress you up nice and not too sexy."

Rainbow scowled but Will held up his hand and said:

"Wait on, Rainbow, let me get through. One minute you'll wear nice stuff so people will think there goes Little Bo Peep, and then next they'll wonder where did Rita Hayworth come from. Might even find a pair of long-sleeve gloves that fit real tight and come halfway up your arms like I see a lot of stars wear. Ain't that right, Leroy?"

Leroy nodded.

Rainbow said: "You really mean it about them long-sleeve gloves, Leroy? Real kid gloves?"

"Just like Will says."

Rainbow won the title of Miss Crappie in white kid gloves and as a redhead, but it was the bathing suit competition that did it. There was no talent contest to speak of. Rainbow did a little dance and that was all. She won on a fine summer night when the sweet smell of honeysuckle was in the air and the sky was so full of moon you could hardly see the stars. There was some talk of holding a run-off with the rival Miss Bass, but the bass people said no. Miss Bass was a blonde from DeWitt who was a little swayback and knobby-kneed, and she couldn't hold a light to Rainbow. It might have been quite a contest, though, because Miss Bass could really sing, but nobody wanted that after they'd seen Rainbow in a bathing suit.

That night everybody piled into A. J.'s pickup and rode around the countryside to celebrate. A. J. had already sold the boat for $100 and they had money to burn. They bought beer and whiskey and ice and hit the road. Will, Thurmond, Pepper, and Pierpont were in the back, and Rainbow was up front between A. J. and Leroy. They had their instruments and they played music and sang. Even Rainbow sang, loudly and terribly. Will was standing against the back window, yodeling and playing his guitar so hard his thumb started to bleed. Thurmond was wild on his drums and every time he rapped his cymbals it sounded like a Chinese invasion. Pepper was thumping his bass fiddle with his eyes closed and the scroll was sticking out of the side of the truck. Pierpont sang and drank with the rest and every once in a while he would lift up his head and scream. Pierpont was drunk out of his mind.

As A. J. drove on through the night, the beer cans flew and the boys howled. An awful noise came from the truck. Lights in houses along the road came on when they passed by, dogs hit the ditch, and other drivers pulled way over when they saw them coming down the road. It was a fine night and they made music. They played and sang some wild songs and some sweet ones, too: "I Can't Stand Myself If You Can't Stand Me," and "Swamp Rat," and "Freight Train," and "That Lucky Old Sun," and old, old, "Peg O' My Heart."

Leroy threw out a beer can and whooped: "Oh, man, what I wouldn't give to be on the flip side of ol' Peg!" The can pinged on the pavement and shot scraping onto the gravel shoulder and tumbled down into a ditch and sank slowly in a muddy pool of water.

Outside of Monroe, they saw an old hobo walking along the highway, and A. J. hit the brakes hard and scrambled a lot of shoulder gravel. A. J. jumped out and ran over to the man.

"Where you going, mister? We'll give you a ride."

"Get away from me!" The man looked blinded and his face was white in the headlights.

Leroy got out and came over, and Rainbow swung out on the door.

A. J. grabbed the man's hand and shook it. "We're heading up the road. Maybe as far as Marianna. We'll give you a ride."

"I don't want to go to Marianna."

"Sure you do, man. Come on and get in."

They made their arms into a seat and swooped him up and carried him to the truck like a native king. They put him up front and Rainbow sat on his lap with her arm around his neck. They sang to him for twenty miles and tried to get him to take a drink. But the guy wouldn't drink and he wouldn't sing. He was scared to death.

Outside of Marianna, A. J. stopped at Lex's Pit Stop Bar B Q and hauled the man over to the window. There was a girl inside and she didn't know what to make of it. A. J. studied the girl seriously and told her:

"This gent is a friend of mine and he wants four dollars worth of cheeseburgers." A. J. gave her four dollars.

The girl could smell the liquor. She looked at A. J. and kind of smiled: "You don't want no milk or coffee, anything like that, do you?"

"What about it, Boyd?" The guy's name was Boyd something.

"Goddammit, leave me alone!"

A. J. winked at the girl. "He's so tired and hungry he don't know a thing he's saying. But you take care of old Boyd. You hear?" And he went back to the pickup and drove away leaning on the horn.

Later that night, A. J. pulled off the road onto a sandy beach along the St. Francis River that was thick with willows and sycamores. There, they built a fire and drank whiskey and sang a lot more songs and finally they sang themselves to sleep. Pepper lovingly made himself a pillow of sand down by the water. Thurmond was nearly under a sycamore tree, and Rainbow and Leroy lay close to the died-out fire. A. J. and Pierpont were in the back of the truck, and A. J. had hold of Will's guitar. His fingers gripped the frets and he strummed lightly on the strings. He made a sound that was almost music but it wasn't quite. The tune wasn't there. He looked at Pierpont and said:

"I always wanted to play one of these things. Thought I might be able to pick it up as much as I've heard." He shook his head.

Pierpont looked at him closely. "Why don't you take a lesson?"

"Have. But I can't get it. Don't have the touch."

Then he put his head down and went to sleep. Off somewhere, Will was yodeling softly.

11

THE NEXT MORNING the earth was heavy with dew. The pickup windows were blinded with it, and the leaves of the willows and sycamores hung limp and wet. Fog nuzzled in close to the ground. Rainbow and the boys had not moved, and they were hidden below the layer of fog. It was as thick as cotton, but a man could stand above it.

Pepper was the first to awake, and when he came up out of that fog, he looked like something from a Count Dracula movie. Pepper could have been the Count. His face was pasty and his eyes were saggy and moribund and bleary from a tremendous headache.

Leroy heard him stumbling around, and he sat up with just his head sticking out of the fog. Pepper almost stepped on him and jumped back with a little scream. Leroy frowned, put back his head sleepily, and vanished beneath the fog. Pepper tiptoed over to the pickup, looking for the beer cooler. He felt a desperate thirst.

Pepper had never been much of a drinker, but he always tried. He did his best to hold it, and when he couldn't, he was ashamed of himself. He could never understand how he could eat all those peppers and still not have a stomach for whiskey. A. J. had told him that the secret of being a good drinker was to use lots of ice, and Pepper used more than anybody, but he finished faster because of that, and his drinks mounted up. It wasn't long until he would be plastered to the point that he'd crawl right in with a hog and think he was between satin sheets.

Pepper was sorry now that he had held it all the night before. He crawled into the back of the truck and kneeled down beside the beer cooler and dipped his head inside. The ice had melted, but the water was still cold and felt wonderful on his clammy face.

He turned around and sat there, trying not to breathe too deeply because of the chest pains. A. J. and Pierpont didn't wake up. Then, little things like tadpoles started swimming in front of Pepper's eyes, and his head felt hot. He closed his eyes and rubbed them gently with his fingertips. They were swollen and grainy. That's when he noticed something about his tongue. It didn't feel right. He wiggled it around, pulled it out with his finger and tried to see it.

Pepper jumped down from the truck, and he was scared. Acne was bad enough, but what was this? He started to sweat. He banged on the rear fender hoping that A. J. would get up. He didn't. So Pepper banged again. Still, nobody was moving. Pepper walked over to where he thought Leroy had risen out of the fog and felt down through it like a man searching for his shoes in the middle of the night.

"Leroy," he called softly, but his voice was shrill and quaked a little. He patted his hand on the ground, feeling. "Leroy," he called louder. "I got to talk to you about something. Where are you, Leroy?"

"Dammit, Pepper," Leroy said from somewhere under the fog. "Will you shut up and go to sleep?"

"Sun's high, Leroy. It's real high," Pepper said and stooped under the fog, following the sound of the voice like a detective.

Leroy growled. "It's dark and cool down here and I aim to keep sleeping a while. Don't feel too good and don't want to talk."

"That's what I need to do, Leroy. I got to talk to you."

Leroy refused to answer. From under his sycamore tree, Thurmond rose up and called Pepper a bad name and then retired into the misty oblivion. Will had not been heard from, but somewhere under the canvas of fog came a whistling kind of snoring with a throaty warble, like you might expect from a yodeler.

Pepper's voice was pleading. "Leroy!"

Leroy grunted and sat up. His eyes were bloodshot and angry. "Well, what?"

"Look here," Pepper said crawling over with his mouth open. He was pointing inside with quick, little jabs.

"Don't see a thing," Leroy said.

"You got to look closer." Leroy did and frowned. "Can't you even find it?" Pepper's voice cracked again.

"Find what, for Chrissakes? You think I'm a dentist?"

"It ain't that, Leroy, it's my tongue. Oh, Lord, my tongue's gone and shrunk up on me! It feels little!" Pepper was trembling badly.

"I don't see nothing the matter with your tongue."

"It sure feels funny. Are you sure?"

"It looks about the regular size to me. Wish it wasn't. Go back to sleep."

"Leroy, I'd sure appreciate it if Rainbow was to let me have her mirror so I can check it."

Leroy was disgusted. "I ain't gonna wake Rainbow so you can look at your tongue."

"You damn right you ain't!" Rainbow said from under the fog.

"Go look in the mirror in the pickup," Leroy told him.

"Aw," Pepper said. "Didn't think of that."

"Well, go on!"

Pepper went back to the truck and slid across the front seat and contemplated himself in the mirror with his mouth closed. Suddenly, he stuck out his tongue, all the way, hard and straining and making a terrible face. He held it long enough for his back jaws to hurt. But when he got out of the truck he was smiling.

"Hey, you guys! Leroy! It's all right. It ain't shrunk up on me after all!"

There was not a sound from the others, and the fog lay thick and heavy over the ground.

"Well, it's all right anyway," Pepper said, and there was a note of sadness in his voice. He went back to the place where he had spent the night, looked around once to see if anyone had risen, and then sat down and lay back slowly and disappeared.

It was about noon. The boys sat in a row just off shore with their heads sticking out of the water like a string of buoys. Their bodies were still hot with whiskey and their faces were scarlet with hangover shine. The river was a little muddy and not cold enough to cause a shudder in a great grandmother, but the boys were shivering.

Rainbow was further downstream bathing in the brown water and not liking the feel of mud between her toes. After a while, she came out and put on her skirt behind a willow tree. Then she walked over to the pickup with nothing else on, finished dressing in the front seat and started honking the horn for the others to get out.

They drove back to Clarendon to get Leroy's car, and A. J. was taking the curves real easy. Everybody wore sunglasses. Nobody said much. Rainbow was up front with Leroy. The others were in the back, each one in his own corner.

When they were coming across the bridge into town, A. J. said: "Rainbow, me and Leroy talked it over. It's time you had some singing lessons."

"Yeah?" Her tone was slightly belligerent.

A. J. took a matchbook cover from his shirt pocket and looked at it. "Molly wrote down a guy's name. Julio Rubini over in Memphis. Molly says he's good. I'll call him and we'll go see Julio tomorrow."

"I don't want to." She looked at Leroy.

Leroy was acting like he was asleep, letting A. J. handle this.

Rainbow nudged him. "Hey, possum! You. Leroy!" She took his glasses off.

Leroy opened one eye. "Do like he says," he told her wearily. "That contest in Batesville is less than two weeks off. You'll have to show some talent this time."

"Talent's ass."

"We'll get you some new clothes in Memphis," A. J. said.

"Well, all right then."

They got to Memphis the next morning and spent an hour and $150 in Levy's buying Rainbow four new outfits. One was a sheath with a Spanish-style neckline and a skirt that fit like house paint. She was wearing that when they walked into the dining room of the Peabody Hotel to eat lunch and on the chance that Doodle Socket might be there. He was.

Doodle Socket always came into the Peabody dining room at least once a day when he was in Memphis to drink coffee and be seen. That day he was wearing a purple shirt with a white ruff and green pants that came down to the floor and covered his elevator shoes. He had his dark glasses on and was sitting at a table by himself. His legs were crossed, and when people came in, he looked at them with a brief and incomparably remote sneer.

A. J. and Leroy got the same treatment when they came in with Rainbow and the others, so they let Doodle sit by himself. "Who does he think he is anyway?" Rainbow said. "Piss on him!"

Leroy waved to the headwaiter, Charles, a tall, thicknecked man, as they sat down. Charles didn't care for Leroy and the Highway 70 Six. He frowned, straightened his blue serge coat and lifted his head imposingly as if he was about to be photographed or shot as a martyr to his country. It was hard to tell which. Leroy had once referred to Charles as the head butler, and Charles had never forgiven him. He didn't know A. J. or Pierpont, but he didn't like them either. They were with Leroy. That was enough.

Charles moved over to their table slowly and circled it like a dog going around a bush. Leroy and the others swung their heads to keep him in sight, and pretty soon Charles had to say something. His tone was snide and impatient.

"You people going to order iced tea and eat the crackers or do you want a real dinner?"

Usually, the band ate at the Krystal Grill across the street. You could get a Krystal hamburger for a dime. They were forty cents in the Peabody dining room. So when they came to the Peabody they just had iced tea, and they did go through the crackers.

Leroy looked hurt: "Chuck!"

Charles scowled. The name Chuck was not his style. He had blue-grey hair and wore $60 suits, and he had taken voice lessons to lose his country accent. But that blue serge was just a little too tight across his chest and maybe a hair short at the wrists. Leroy always said he looked like Frankenstein.

Charles said with dignity, "The name is Charles."

"Chuck Turley," Leroy introduced him to A. J. "From over in Snowball."

"Howdy, Chuck."

"Yeah," Rainbow said, "and he's as country as greens."

Charles reddened. There are some things you just can't hide or that won't go away. It had kept him out of a big hotel in St. Louis and he couldn't get the job he really wanted in New Orleans. Even at the Peabody they just let him work the day shift. Charles was a pretty good headwaiter, but he'd never go any higher than Memphis.

"I'll get you a waitress," Charles said.

"Wait a minute before you go," Leroy said. He pointed over to Doodle Socket. "That's our headliner over there. You know, the guy in dark glasses who acts like he's Tyrone Power. Doodle Socket Purvis."

"The one who's dressed up like a rooster?"

"That's him. Well, we ain't speaking right now, so I wonder if you'd take him a message?"

"I look like a Western Union boy?"

"Where's your bicycle, Chuck?" Will said.

Charles walked away without a word but his fists were clenched.

Leroy wrote the message on a slip of paper, and the waitress took it over. The note said: "Rainbow won the Miss Crappie contest. Sold a $100 boat they gave as a prize. Blew some on whiskey, etc. The rest goes for Rainbow's singing lessons. Did Ed Sullivan ever call? If not see you at Molly's."

He signed it Cecil B. DeMille.

Doodle Socket wadded up the note with one hand and dropped it in his water glass. It floated nicely. He eased out of his chair and rose on his tiptoes and then came down again and started across the room. He moved slowly and smiled, a thin, gunfighter's smile like Jack Palance just before Alan Ladd blows his head off in *Shane*. He stopped beside Leroy and said:

"Singing lessons for Rainbow? That's a crock." He laughed.

Rainbow got up fast and Doodle Socket backed off a step or two.

"Take it easy, Rainbow," Leroy said.

Rainbow said: "You watch your mouth, short stuff, before I knock you off them elevator shoes."

Doodle Socket couldn't take that. He started around the table after Rainbow. She was going to meet him half way, but A. J. grabbed Doodle and held him off the floor. His feet were still moving like a wind-up toy but he had no traction. A. J. carried him out of the dining room and into the lobby before he set him down.

A. J. said: "Go get your T-Bird, Doodle Socket. We'll see you in Marked Tree. Drive fast and cool off."

"God damn you anyway!" Doodle Socket said. He was still mad and he spat on the ducks in the fountain on his way out.

In the dining room, Leroy was trying to calm Rainbow down. Charles came over. "What's the trouble here?"

"Just a little argument, Chuck."

"Don't call me 'Chuck.' I don't like it."

Leroy and Rainbow took their seats. Leroy said: "To tell you the truth, I don't either."

"None of us do," Will said.

"We all hate it," Thurmond said.

"It stinks," Pepper said.

Charles blinked at them a moment and then went back to his station.

They finished lunch, a real lunch of roast beef, mashed potatoes, and peas, and on the way out Leroy stopped at the door and slipped Charles a tip. The way Leroy handled it, it looked like he was going to give him a dollar, but it was only a quarter. Charles smiled as he took it, and then realized it was just a quarter. He didn't have to see it to know. He could feel it and it was a quarter. He stood there clenching his fist until his knuckles were white and his fingers hurt. He hated that quarter but he kept it.

Leroy, who had had enough of Rainbow for one day, and the boys went to the show to see John Wayne and Montgomery Clift in *Red River*, and A. J. and Pierpont took Rainbow out to Mr. Rubini's for her singing lesson. Julio lived in a pretty nice neighborhood that had sidewalks and a lot of trees. Julio was waiting for them in his front yard under a mimosa tree in a swinging lounge that had a tasseled awning and was designed with orange flowers. Julio lay full length on the swing. He wore a Hawaiian shirt and shorts that came down to his knees and sandals with yellow socks. Julio was fat and he was sweating even though he was in the shade.

Rainbow waited to one side while A. J. talked to Julio about money. The price was $25, but Julio said: "You no can expect me to teach her in a-one easy lesson. You take-a your chances, mister."

A. J. said fine. "Just give her a few pointers, Julio. Do the best you can."

Rainbow went into the house with Mr. Rubini. A. J. and Pierpont stayed outside. They sat on the swing and listened to Julio playing the scales and to Rainbow lifting her voice in pitiful song. It was bad. A man and his wife who were playing cards in their yard next door got up and went inside. Some dogs started howling down the block. A. J. could see windows closing in nearby houses.

The music continued. Rainbow had plenty of volume, but no tone and no pitch. Her high notes sounded like squealing tires. Rainbow would reach the top of the scale, Julio would shout something, and they would start over again. Once, there was a pause and the sound of a crash inside.

Pierpont got up and began pacing the yard. He looked nervously toward the house. "I am beginning to have second thoughts about this beauty pageant."

"You were all for it there a while back."

Pierpont shook his head. "Not any more. No good will come of it. You can mark my words."

Inside, Rainbow was singing again.

After about thirty minutes, the music stopped and the house was quiet. It stayed quiet for another five minutes and still no music. A. J. went inside to investigate and Pierpont tagged along. The front door was unlocked. A. J. went down the hall, calling as he went. He found Rainbow and Julio in the music room in the back of the house.

Rainbow was sitting on the piano with her legs crossed like a torch singer, but her head was bowed and she was leaning back on her hands. She looked exhausted. A broken vase of flowers lay on the floor.

A. J. tried to sound cheerful. "How's it going?"

Julio was in a corner sunk in a large easy chair. He was sweating and breathing hard and his eyes were wide open and vacant. Rainbow slipped off the piano and tiptoed over to A. J.

"I ain't too good, Kid," she whispered. "Come on, let's get out of here. He's done cried twice."

12

THEY WERE SITTING in Molly's office at the Shake Loose, and everybody had a seat except Doodle Socket and Shade. Rainbow had Molly's sofa all to herself, and she was stretched out polishing her nails. Doodle was leaning against the wall, eyeing Rainbow sourly. Shade stood by the door. A. J. said:

"We can forget Rainbow as a singer. Maybe there's something else she can do."

Molly looked her over. "I remember once when I was Miss Poinsett County. Allison Sanders went all the way to the semifinals and all she did was twirl a baton. She wasn't half as good looking as Rainbow. Think you could pick it up, girl?"

"I learn fast," Rainbow said.

Doodle Socket chuckled: "Might get her a broomstick and let her twirl up a storm."

"What you talking about a broomstick? I'm warning you!"

A. J. led Doodle to one side and told him if he didn't lay off Rainbow he'd take his car keys away. A. J. meant it and Doodle Socket knew it. "OK. OK."

Shade got a mop out of the closet. He broke the handle with his fingers like a pretzel, took out his knife and whittled off the splinters and handed it to Rainbow without a word.

"Why thanks, Shade." She got up and started practicing. "Good," Molly said and then told them she had some news. Most of the sponsors she'd talked to, Flossie, and Blackie, and Stoplight, were going to be in Batesville for the contest, though there was some doubt about Billy Luke because of his hernia.

"How'd that happen?"

"Tried to lift a beer bottle and couldn't."

They all had to know how you got a hernia trying to lift a beer bottle, and Molly said:

"Because old Spider Coombs had hold of it. That's right. You all know Spider. Well, the other night him and Billy Luke fell to arguing over this and that, and when Billy Luke reached for the bottle, Spider must of thought he was going to get brained. So he put his hand around it and said no.

"Billy Luke is pretty stout, too. He grabbed hold of the neck and gave it a big pull and then he took it with both hands and first thing you know he's up on the table pulling on that bottle with his arms between his legs. That's when it popped on him. One of the boys said it sounded just like a cork coming out of a bottle of whiskey."

Everybody had a beer on that, and then they had another one because the beers were cold and free. They stayed the rest of the week in Marked Tree and picked up some extra money playing nights at the Shake Loose. Rainbow, however, did not put in an appearance. She stayed in the motel and practiced with a real baton they had bought her in town. After a few days, her figure eights and hand-over-hands were perfect and she could do a high toss with six revolutions and only drop it once in a while.

"It ain't as easy as it looks," Rainbow announced. "This baton twirling takes real talent."

Everybody said "sure."

They left for Batesville Sunday afternoon. A. J. had called Doris about putting them up, and Doris had said fine. It was raining when they got to town.

They drove across the causeway to the White River bridge, and the sky was squirrel grey and dripping. The clouds reached all the way to the ground, and some of them, whiter than the others, rose up in shredded columns like renegade ghosts and hung in the air. The river was almost invisible below.

It was dark when they got to Doris and Joe's. They climbed the walk to the front porch, and A. J. hammered the door knocker.

Doris was sitting by the front window with her head buried in *True Detective*, and she was eating shelled peanuts with ferocious speed. She jumped when the knocker sounded and looked up with her eyes wide open and wild as if the Hooded Terror was right there in the room.

She sat very still for a moment with only her jaws moving, and then she wiped a hole in the window and saw A. J. and the others on the porch shaking themselves like dogs. Doris put down her *True Detective* with its strangled cover girl and went to the door. She threw it open and welcomed A. J. with open arms.

"Come in the house," she said. "It's good to have company on a stormy night." She swept them all in with movements of her arms like she was rolling tires. "I got a hen in the pot and bread in the oven and whiskey for later. Make yourselves at home." Then she lowered her voice and spoke confidentially to A. J. "Joe'll be right down. They all know about him?"

A. J. nodded.

"Good." She went to the foot of the stairs and yelled up. "Joe! The train's come in!"

"How's he been doing lately?" A. J. asked.

"Fine. No problems." And she winked at A. J. "The railroad's been running without a hitch ever since you left."

Upstairs, a door opened and closed, and Joe, dressed in his black uniform and wearing his conductor's hat, appeared at the top of the landing. He came down the stairs slowly and with dignity.

"Seventeen minutes late," he said, checking his huge pocket watch. "But she'll make up time between here and Little Rock. Everything is running smooth up and down the line." He closed the metal guard over the face of the watch with a snap and looked everyone in the eye as if expecting an argument. Nobody said a word.

Joe nodded seriously and moved over in front of Rainbow. "So, this is our beauty queen. It's a pleasure to have you riding with us, young lady." He bent down, giving her one of those Old World bows, and then he kissed her and straightened up. He shook A. J.'s hand and said, "Welcome aboard, Kid." Then he looked at Doris. "If supper is ready, Doris Lou-

Ann, let's eat. It's late. We'll have the diner to ourselves."

Joe held out his arms to Doris and Rainbow and led them slowly into the dining room.

The next morning the sky was clear and the trees and grass were green and shining after the rain. Registration was at two o'clock that afternoon at the Powell Motel. The first official event was set for Tuesday night when the girls would all be introduced at a banquet at the American Legion Hall, and that was to be followed by a dance.

Rainbow was up early. She kept saying she wanted to take a look at that $1,500 mink coat. It was on display at Thorndike's Department Store. A. J. and Leroy put her off until about nine, then drove downtown. Pierpont went with them. On the way they swung by the river where the beauty pageant and other events in the carnival like the motorboat races, the swimming meet, the fishing derby, and the watermelon eating contest, would be held. The watermelon eating contest was still part of the festival but it wasn't a big deal anymore. At the river, workmen were building a floating platform and stage just off shore for the beauty queens and the watermelon eaters and were setting up bleachers along the bank. There was a lot of room for extra chairs.

On a grassy vacant lot up the hill from the stands, another crew was raising a large tent that belonged to Dr. G. Gerald Evans' revival group. Gerald was a healing evangelist working out of Enid, Oklahoma. In front of where the tent was going up a van was parked with a sign in large letters that said:

Dr. G. Gerald Evans
World Famous Evangelist
God Not Chance! The Healing Faith!

The revival was to start Wednesday and last through Sunday.

Outside of Thorndike's front window, Rainbow stood looking at the mink coat. Her eyes were narrow with greed and hope. The coat was fitted over a headless mannequin, and it was a full-length dandy that touched the floor.

Pierpont said: "That is indeed a fine piece of fur."

Rainbow closed her eyes and said softly, prayerfully: "If I win it, I promise I'll never take it off."

Leroy snorted, "You going to sleep in it, too?"

Rainbow's eyes popped open and she stuck out her chin. "I might!"

Later that morning, they went by Steve Best's Quality Photography Studio on Main Street, and Rainbow sat for some pictures to give to the papers. Steve was a swarthy man with slick, black hair and long, delicate fingers and shiny nails. The studio smelled of some kind of incense, which Leroy said he thought was part coon. The furniture was modern and stripey, and there was a thick rug on the floor that showed footprints.

Rainbow was in back with Steve for nearly an hour. The pictures weren't cheap. Steve said they would be $50, including tax.

Leroy looked at Rainbow: "You're expensive, gal."

Rainbow grinned. "I'm worth it. Huh, Steve?"

Steve looked uncomfortable. He folded his hands together and his fingernails flashed in the light.

"Your pictures will be ready tomorrow," Steve said, then slipped through the door to the back.

Leroy looked suspiciously at Rainbow. "What went on back there?"

Rainbow said: "Nothing much. He said 'how about a bare-chest shot or two' and I said 'fine.'"

"You didn't!" Leroy said.

"Sure. Why not? He give me ten dollars."

"God damn, Rainbow," A. J. said. "That was dumb. What if somebody got hold of them shots?"

"Don't worry about it."

Outside, Pierpont whispered to A. J. "I told you, Kid. I told you."

They took Rainbow to the Powell at two o'clock to register. Rainbow was wearing a pink and white cotton suit and she said she felt wonderful.

"Well, don't do anything else dumb," Leroy told her.

The contest headquarters was just down from the lobby.

The producer was a woman named Viola Summerall and she had a suite of rooms outside of which was a desk and a sign that said:

Welcome, Girls

A rainbow trout and a largemouth bass with crossed American and Arkansas flags between was painted below the words.

Miss Summerall was a large woman with skinny legs that tapered down to her ankles like sharpened pencils. Her hair was dyed orange and she wore a red suit and an orchid. She smiled at Rainbow and told her to come along. "We'll have a little talk and you can meet some of the other girls."

"Pleased to."

That was all that happened Monday.

Tuesday night, everybody came down to the Legion Hall. The place was packed. There were twenty-five girls in the pageant and they sat at special tables with their parents and sponsors. The legion commander, Theo Nelson, a World War I cavalry officer, read the names of the girls from a slip of paper and said where they were from and who their mothers and fathers were. The girls got up, one by one, and bowed. Everybody clapped.

Most of them were good looking but a few were outstanding. Miss Little Red River and Miss Crooked Creek, for example, but you couldn't count out Miss Perch or Miss Trout or Miss Spring River. A. J. and Leroy were worried most about Miss Little Red, Emily Ann Thalmueller from Greers Ferry. Emily Ann had canary-blonde hair, a large mouth, and a glittering smile. She had poise and knew exactly what she was doing because she had had experience as a tomato princess.

Some of the other girls knew right away when Miss Little Red stood up proudly, arched her shoulders back and let her smile sweep the room like a spotlight, that they were out of the running. Miss Sunfish, Clare Wormser from Newport, looked at her father across the table and she was ready to cry. Mr. Wormser put his hand on hers, but he was frowning. The applause for Miss Little Red was thunderous and some of the people whistled and stamped their feet before she sat down.

Rainbow did all right. When Theo introduced her, she got up slowly, like a curl of smoke rising, and did a perfect stand and a complete turn. She got good applause, but it was nothing next to Miss Little Red's. Even Miss Crooked Creek got more. And nobody had whistled or stamped their feet for Rainbow.

Later that night, A. J. had a conference with Leroy and then called Molly in Marked Tree. He told her five or six roadhouse people wouldn't do for a rooting section. They needed a busload. What could she do? Molly said she'd see. Maybe some of the guys from the Lepanto–Marked Tree VFW could come and bring their wives. She and Shade would look into it. And she said she'd call Billy Luke over in Trumann. She said Billy Luke was doing all right now, though he still stooped a little when he walked.

The next morning, A. J. got a call from a man named Bobby Gene Boosey. When A. J. hung up, he looked at Leroy.

"This guy wants me to come down to the river and have a little talk. About noon. Says he's a friend of Steve Best, the photographer."

"Oh, shit!"

To get to the meeting place, A. J. had to drive across the White River bridge, turn back on a dirt road that ran through a field of hay, and then follow it along what was a lovers' lane in low water. The sun was high and hot, but it was cool along the river, and A. J. could hear the quail calling in the woods beyond the field. Some people were fishing from the bank, some standing and others sitting with their backs rested against trees.

Bobby Gene was driving a 1953 white-over-blue Mercury. A couple of pieces of the grill were missing and the sides were stained with mud. Bobby Gene was behind the wheel sucking Sen-Sen. He was a weaselly man with a pinched face and sharp teeth. He wore a purple sheen suit that shined like radium paint and black and white shoes. He had a pint of Four Roses in his hip pocket.

Bobby Gene had quick, nervous hands and a slow smile, but it was a shadowy smile and there was a hard light in his eyes. A. J. noticed he had tiny holes in his teeth like the black spots on dice. His face was vaguely familiar, but A. J. couldn't place it. Bobby Gene got out of the car.

"Mr. Poole? Glad you could make it." He sized A. J. up. "You look like a pretty smart fella to me."

A. J. didn't say anything and Bobby Gene went on. "I won't keep you. No, like I said on the phone, Steve Best is a friend of mine. I've done him some favors. Well, according to old Steve, this Rainbow Wimberly of yours don't care what kind of pictures people take of her."

"Go on."

"No, she really don't. And you know something else? I seen this Rainbow some place. Believe it was over there in Lepanto. Roadhouse they call Flossie's. Heard a rumor or two about Rainbow and this old boy named Leroy, uh, Scroggins? 'Course, I didn't think nothing about it at the time."

"I getcha. How much is it gonna cost us?"

Bobby Gene's eyes flashed and he smiled, exposing that row of sharp teeth. "Well, now, you move fast. Two hunnerd dollars. That's all. A hunnerd for me and likewise for good old Steve."

"That's a lot of money, Bobby Gene!"

"I understand how you feel. You think about it some. I do want to say, though, it ain't all that much considering them prizes. No, sir."

"We'll have to talk it over."

"You do that. You can meet me here, say, about one o'clock tomorrow?" He lifted the Four Roses from his pocket and took a drink and then offered the bottle to A. J.

A. J. skipped the whiskey and said: "You may not appreciate this, but how do we know we can trust you and good old Steve?"

"Aw, man, you'll get them pictures back. Sure you won't have a slug of this Four Roses? Do you good."

A. J. told the others in Doris' living room and Doodle Socket slammed his fist on his knee so hard that the nerve got pinched and his leg jerked out against a table, spilling a bottle of Falstaff beer. No one picked up the bottle.

"We won't pay it!" Doodle Socket said.

Rainbow looked at him fiercely. "Well, I ain't going to quit!"

Joe was so mad he stood up grandly in his uniform, took off his conductor's hat, and bit down on the hard, black bill with all the force of his jaws. His teeth made a perfect half circle C, and then he sailed his hat into the dining room. He was shaking, but he was all right. Doris went over and stood beside him.

Will jumped up and said: "I'll find that shutterbug and fix his ass! We'll get them pictures back." He started for the door.

"I'm coming, too!" Pepper cried.

Rainbow was holding her baton like a baseball bat. "Let me do it," she said and started after them.

"Wait a minute!" Leroy shouted. "Come back here. Let's talk this over." They stopped at the door and Leroy looked at A. J. "Got any ideas, Kid?"

"Nothing sensational. And I got to let him know tomorrow."

Then they noticed that Thurmond was acting strangely. He was pacing over by the window, scratching his head and mumbling to himself. Finally, he stopped pacing and looked at the others nervously. He said:

"Did I ever tell you about the screwdaddle wampus?"

"The what?"

"The screwdaddle wampus."

"What's that?"

"One of them concoctions." Thurmond scratched his head again. "If I can just remember it."

"What's it do?"

"I can remember that! You get hold of some and you'll go to ranting and raving and plumb take loose of your senses. I mean it. You won't make a bit of sense. Had a uncle once took some by accident—I heard it was a accident—and he flat didn't know his own wife for the better part of a month.

If I can just think what was in it."

They all agreed that the screwdaddle wampus might be just the thing for Bobby Gene. Steve Best, too, for that matter. They sat Thurmond down on Doris' sofa and tried to help him remember. They made him comfortable. Doris brought him a pair of Joe's slippers and eased them on his feet. Rainbow got behind him and started rubbing his shoulders, softly, soothingly. Thurmond said that helped.

"Come on, Thurm, you got to try harder."

"I'm trying!"

Doris made him some hot chicken broth and served it on a tray, and Doodle Socket gave him a concert of sweet, pretty songs, mellow and nostalgic. When Rainbow wasn't rubbing his shoulders, she twirled her baton, sensuously, hypnotically. They had to shake Thurmond about noon to keep him from dozing off.

"Don't go to sleep on us, Thurm."

"Don't sleep now, boy."

"I'm trying to think."

"That's it. That's the way."

Pepper was standing by with pad and pencil to write down what Thurmond was going to think of. A. J. took him by the arm. "You're the pharmacist here, Pepper, you got to help him think."

"Don't have much to go on, Kid."

"Well, get your book out."

About one o'clock, Thurmond sat up straight on the sofa and said: "Dillweed. Yeah. That's part of it. And dry mustard." Then he fell back. "But there's a whole lot else and I just can't think of it."

"Keep trying, Thurm."

"Don't give up."

"We're with you all the way."

"A little whiskey might help."

Leroy went down to the car and came back with a bottle of Jack Daniel's Black Label. Nothing but the best for Thurmond. Thurmond had the first drink and they passed the bottle around. Rainbow was rubbing Thurmond's shoulders again. Doodle Socket was still singing quietly.

At one-thirty, Thurmond had a false alarm. He rose up, his eyes narrowed and gleaming, and for an instant he stopped breathing. Then he slumped again, shaking his head. He looked exhausted. They gave him some more Jack Daniels and at two o'clock sharp, Thurmond began to smile and his breathing came fast.

"It's coming back! It's coming! I keep thinking of frogs. Oh, why in the world are them frogs in there?"

Will made a sound like a frog: "Wa-rump. Wa-rump. Wa-rump."

"That's good, Will," Thurmond said. "Keep it up. It's coming back and I ain't lying. Oh, yeah. Oh, yeah. Wait a minute. I got it! You got to have a bullfrog's belly, cut and dry as a bone. And you make it into a powder, real fine. And wait a minute. There's a cat in there somewhere. I'm thinking of cats now."

"Some catnip?" Pepper said breathlessly.

Thurmond looked at him and said: "Pepper, you are a true genius. That's it. That's it, boys. About an ounce of catnip and we're in business!"

Everybody slapped Thurmond on the back. Rainbow gave him a kiss, and Doodle Socket stopped singing. Pepper read off the recipe from his notes. A pinch of dillweed, a pinch of dry mustard, one frog's belly, cut and dried into a powder, and an ounce of catnip.

Then they were all surprised to see Thurmond frown. He looked crestfallen. "But that ain't all. There's something else. Oh, Lord, something I forgot."

"Well, come on, Thurmond!"

"What is it?"

"Let me have some more of that black Jack."

Thurmond was a little drunk now. His eyes were beginning to glaze. His tongue and his cheeks burned. "There was some kind of acid in it, too."

"Oh, no!" Pierpont said.

"We don't want to kill him, Thurmond," A. J. said.

"Why not?" Rainbow said savagely.

"Help him out there, Pepper," Leroy said. "Look in your book. What kind of acid?"

Pepper went down the list: Alizorin. Boric. Boron. Cloride. Halide. Lysergic. Nitric . . .

"Wait on there! Did you say lysergic? That's it, boys. Yes, sir. Now you got your screwdaddle wampus!"

"Hot damn!"

They gave him the Jack Daniels, and Thurmond killed the rest of it. Then his eyelids fluttered closed and he passed out cold as an axe blade.

The boys went bullfrog hunting and after an hour or so had brought in two nice big ones. They found all the dry mustard they needed in a field across the river. Pierpont and Rainbow got the lysergic acid downtown, and as it turned out, Doris was growing dill and catnip in her backyard. It was just about dark when everyone got back.

The next morning, they were all up at first light to catch the early sun so the frog's stomach would be completely dry by one. It was ready by noon and Doris made the powder and Thurmond mixed the potion. Shortly before one o'clock, A. J. set off for his appointment with Bobby Gene, and he was carrying a pint of Jack Daniels laced with the screwdaddle wampus in his back pocket. Thurmond, Doodle Socket, and Pierpont followed in Doris' car—at a distance.

Pepper and Will rode with Leroy downtown. Leroy parked the car in the alley behind Steve's photography shop and walked around the corner and came in the front. Pepper and Will went in the back door.

A couple of minutes later, Leroy held the back door and Steve came out in the alley walking on his tiptoes, trying to get even with his arm Will had twisted behind his back. Steve's teeth were clenched and he was sort of looking over his right shoulder at the source of the pain.

Will shoved Steve into Steve's car and got behind the wheel. Leroy came around to the other side. He held up a roll of negatives and struck a match. The film blazed up brightly and then disappeared in smoke. Leroy got in beside Steve and Will drove out of the alley nice and easy. Pepper followed in Leroy's car. They turned the corner and headed north out of town. When they passed Steve's shop, the shade on the front door was down and a sign in the window said:

CLOSED

Steve was scared. "Where're you taking me?"

Leroy laid a bottle of Jack Daniels on the seat. "We're going to have a little party, Steve baby."

Bobby Gene had parked his car under a sycamore a short distance from the river. He was slouched behind the wheel working on his fingernails with a pocketknife. There were little crescent slivers all over his lap. A large manila envelope lay on the seat beside him. Also a pint of Four Roses. He was reaching for the bottle when he saw A. J. driving along the bank. Bobby Gene checked his watch. It was ten minutes after one.

Bobby Gene opened the door and swung out his feet, but he didn't get out of the car. "You're about on time," he said as A. J. came over. His tone was guarded and edgy, but he smiled when he saw A. J. take an envelope from his pocket.

"Couldn't make it any sooner," A. J. said. He hesitated a moment, then gave Bobby Gene the money.

"I knew you was smart," Bobby Gene said, and handed A. J. the manila in return.

A. J. glanced inside at the pictures and Bobby Gene started counting the money. There were eight twenties and four tens.

"Adds up," Bobby Gene said. He laid the money carefully on the seat.

A. J. put the manila on top of the car and brought out his pint of Jack Daniels. "Thought we'd have a drink and talk a minute," he told Bobby Gene. "See you got your own there, but you might care for a nip of this Old Jack."

Bobby Gene grinned and reached for the Jack Daniels. He handed A. J. his Four Roses. "Here, we'll switch."

"Don't mind if I do."

Bobby Gene raised the bottle of Jack Daniels and took a fine, deep swallow. He got at least two ounces and sighed like a hog.

"That is fine whiskey. What did you want to talk about?"

"Don't be light," A. J. said. "There's plenty there."

Over in the trees, Thurmond, Doodle, and Pierpont watched breathlessly, their faces close together like spying children. Pierpont took Thurmond's arm and gave him a questioning look.

"Any minute," Thurmond said. "It hits 'em fast."

Bobby Gene took another deep drink. "It's got kind of a tangy taste." And Bobby Gene took the car keys out of the slot, got out of the car and threw them as far as he could into the water.

The next thing he did was get down on the ground and cover his face with dirt. He rubbed it on his clothes and up his arms under his sleeves and made streaks in his face. He looked like a headhunter. A. J. was a little afraid of him and backed off. Bobby Gene had gone wild. "Hee. Hee. Hee," he screamed and climbed up on top of his car. Up there, he shouted a stream of curse words and started taking off his pants and then his shirt. He left on his shorts, but that was all. He was still cursing and laughing at the same time. All the fishermen along the river stood up and watched. This was something to see.

Bobby Gene slid down over the trunk and rolled in a mud hole. He looked worse than a coal miner now. He rolled a couple of yards, and when he got up, his eyes were blazing. He sat low in a crouch for a moment, hopped a little way, and then lit out like a cat, shaking his head and screaming: "Hee. Hee. Hee."

Pierpont and Doodle Socket were shaking Thurmond's hand and slapping his back.

"Didn't I tell you?" Thurmond said. He was very proud.

The last they saw of Bobby Gene, he was running up the bank, snatching away peoples' fishing poles and turning their stringers of fish loose in the river. Pretty soon he was running in front of a crowd.

A. J. was looking through Bobby Gene's car when the others came over. Something had caught his eye while he had been drinking the Four Roses.

"Pierpont, look here what I found."

A. J. held up a couple of pilot's helmets and two pairs of goggles.

"Well," Pierpont said, "I will be God damned."

"Look like the same, don't they?" He slipped behind the wheel and read Bobby Gene's address on the white slip in cellophane wrapped around the steering column. He made a note of it and told Thurmond and Doodle Socket they would see them later, they had to make a trip up to Cave City. That's where Bobby Gene lived.

A. J. and Pierpont found Bobby Gene's place at the end of a dirt road about a mile off the blacktop. The house was single story and needed a paint job. There was a stock pond across the road. It was muddy and ringed with an oily slime. Two automobile carcasses were sticking grill-first into the water.

The yard in front of the house was littered with parts of old cars, and chickens were moseying in between the transmissions, scattered gears, and hubs and slick tires. A couple of dogs lay up on the front porch of the house. They got up, stretched and yawned, and came sniffing into the yard. They were skinny and looked hungry.

Around back, the yard was strewn with firewood, discarded furniture, and more car parts. A chicken coop with one side caved in was over on the right. Next to it was a large tin shed. The door to the shed was closed but not locked. A radio was playing inside.

The dogs followed them into the yard, taking aim on the wood or pieces of furniture and then checking to make sure they had hit the right spot. Beyond the shed in a field a lone horse was grazing. It was Superstition Pete's horse, Sonny.

A. J. said: "Go bring him down here, Pierpont. We'll put him in the truck."

A. J. opened the door to the shed quietly. Inside, lying on shelves or mounted on benches and sawhorses were fifteen or twenty outboard motors of all sizes, stacks of tools, some new but most of them used, two or three dozen tackle boxes, rods and reels, jars of lures, and a few cameras. A. J. also counted nine bicycles, seven or eight radios, and five record players scattered around. And there were at least half a dozen sleds hanging from nails on the wall. Also on the wall, was another one of those pilot's helmets and a pair of goggles.

In the back right-hand corner of the shed a man and a girl were sleeping on a cot. They were both dressed but had no shoes on. The girl lay on top, and her arms hung down and dragged the floor. The radio and a bottle of whiskey, almost empty, was on a table by the cot.

A. J. moved quietly. He unscrewed two outboards he thought he recognized as his own. He opened the cowlings and looked underneath the motors. On both of them he found the letters S. L. for his mother's initials. Then he put the cowlings back on and carried the motors outside. Pierpont had come back with Pete's horse.

"Got two of my motors back," A. J. said. "Let's get back to town."

They had to pick Bobby Gene Boosey out of a tall sycamore tree with a fire ladder, and it took two hook and ladders and eight firemen an hour and a half to do it. Bobby Gene was in the very top, swaying on a branch and screaming like a pirate. He was hard to get to that high up, and he kicked and yelled and almost fell once when they were bringing him back to the ground. But he was still screaming and trying to bite, and it took four men in white suits to get him in the ambulance. Bobby Gene spent the rest of the week in a straitjacket in the Batesville Hospital.

Steve Best turned up later that night throwing rocks at store windows on Main Street and finally got arrested for trying to burn down a Baptist church. When they hauled him into the hospital, he kept screaming:

"Don't touch me again or I'll take your picture. You touch me one more time and I'll take your picture. Hee. Hee. Hee. You God damn right I will!"

The cops and the people at the hospital couldn't figure it: two guys with the same kind of crazies in one day? It was peculiar as hell.

13

A. J., RAINBOW, and Leroy walked down Main Street arm in arm, in bright sunshine, and their shadows danced on the store windows and then fell away suddenly in doorways and street corners. They spoke to everybody on the street, and people spoke back. Rainbow was wearing a yellow knit dress, and she stood out like a full moon on a clear night. In her company, Leroy grinned, and A. J. whistled as they walked.

Pierpont on his own had made a call to the sheriff's office, and the cops had picked up Bobby Gene's brother, Ralph, and Ralph's girl friend, Hazel, and confiscated the rest of the loot. For the last two or three years a lot of people had wondered what had happened to their motors and tackle boxes and a lot of kids had missed their radios and bicycles. The cops were waiting for Bobby Gene to come out of it so they could charge him with grand theft. Thurmond said they would have to wait until Sunday anyway and maybe Monday, because it would take that long at least for the screwdaddle wampus to wear off.

A. J. and Leroy escorted Rainbow into Laggett's drugstore and a photographer from the Batesville paper took Rainbow's picture with Mr. Laggett and Elmo the soda jerk. Elmo's jaws were quivering while he posed. Mr. Laggett gave them free Coca-Colas and held the door for them when they left.

Their next stop was at the headquarters of the Rev. Dr. G. Gerald Evans, the healing evangelist. Since the day A. J. had seen Gerald's tent going up, he had been nursing an idea. Molly and Flossie and Billy Luke were due in that afternoon with a busload of Rainbow's faithful from Marked Tree, Lepanto, and Trumann and they would make a pretty good rooting section. But maybe it wouldn't hurt to have a man of the cloth and some ailing Christians on your side, too. A. J. had discussed it with Leroy and Rainbow and had said he wondered if Gerald was anything like his uncle, Buckminster Poole.

Buck had started out as a tent preacher from Brinkley but had gone on to be a radio evangelist and now lived in Phoenix, Arizona, in a big ranch house that had five picture windows and a cross-shaped swimming pool. It was said that he loved black cars and filter cigarettes, and that he was seen occasionally with Elaine Stewart, the movie star.

Gerald had a growing following and a sense of destiny. He had been blinded by sin as a youth of twenty-five but had received his sight one day on the road to Enid, Oklahoma. He was puny at the time; he weighed only 119 pounds and had a mousy voice. He had come up under the tutelage of Buddy "Sweet Chariot" Jordan of Tulsa and had done well enough by now to own his own tent, a tractor-trailer rig to haul it, and a private house trailer. He also boasted an honorary doctorate in religion from Marmaduke College in Riverside, California. The degree had cost forty dollars, but arrived special delivery, and was signed under the seal of the great Homer G. "Pop" Thompson himself, the man, people said, Jesus would most like to see if he were alive today.

Gerald was a tall, limber man, in perfect health—now— and he weighed 175 at least. His hair was thick and heavy and black, and he had a voice that could carry a city block and still be as clear as the sound of a half dollar on a brick-tile floor. Gerald had been saved and he had not forgotten. It was his call to move out through the world on the sawdust trail and bring the other sinners home to God and decency. It was his conviction that sin and infirmity went hand in hand but that when you gave up the one, you could forget about the other.

A. J. nudged Rainbow when they got down to the vacant lot where Gerald's tent was luffing in the breeze. It made little snapping sounds like a popping towel. A. J. said to Rainbow:

"You try and look as sick as you can and let's see what happens."

Rainbow smiled beautifully for an instant, then squinted her eyes in pain and let her shoulders slump.

"Fine," A. J. said. Leroy nodded.

It was a hot afternoon. The door of Gerald's trailer was open to let the breeze come through. Gerald was sitting at a table inside frowning at a sheaf of papers. He held a pencil tightly in his hand. He was absorbed in thought. Suddenly, he started writing, and his pencil scratched furiously across the page. He worked for about a minute with his face close to the paper, which was curled from the pressure of his writing.

When he finished, he got up quickly and walked back to a refrigerator in the rear of the trailer. He took out a bottle of Budweiser that had already been opened and was stopped up with a rubber cap. He flipped up the cap and swallowed the rest of the beer straight down. His Adam's apple bobbed like a cork on the water. Then he held the bottle away from his mouth and let the last foamy drops fall on his tongue. He burped once, then a second time and let it play itself out down to the last semi-sour carbonic gasp and came back to the table hitching his pants.

A. J. knocked on the trailer door. "Afternoon, Dr. Evans. Want you to meet Rainbow Wimberly from Hazen, Arkansas. Rainbow's a beauty queen."

Gerald had never saved a beauty queen before and he was interested.

"Come in, friends," he said, and shook loose some wooden folding chairs with a loud clatter. He and A. J. shook hands. Then he and Leroy. Rainbow sat on the edge of her chair with her knees close together and shining with smoothness like two golden doorknobs. It was just for a moment, but everyone looked at Rainbow's knees.

There were some pamphlets on the table and in stacks on the floor. A. J. picked up "Living in God" and "God's Formula For Success and Prosperity" and one called "Spend Eternity with God" by Dr. Evans that was complete and unabridged in seventeen pages.

"Wouldn't mind reading these sometime," A. J. said and handed another pamphlet to Rainbow that said: "Jesus Never Had an Operation." Rainbow looked inside and studied the contents thoughtfully. A. J. was still holding: "Spend Eternity with God" and thumbing the seventeen pages.

Gerald said: "You go ahead, son. That one you got there is fifty cents. But the others are absolutely free."

"Aw, yeah," A. J. said. "It says fifty cents right there." Gerald smiled, and A. J. put two quarters on the table.

Leroy said: "Reverend Evans, what we come about is Rainbow here. Fact a business is she ain't been feeling at all well lately. Have you gal?"

"Man, that's right." She sounded pretty low.

"Keeps complaining about this clutch pain that just won't quit."

Gerald leaned forward in his chair intently. "Clutch pain?"

Leroy nodded. "It's been on her quite a while now and not a single doctor's been able to help and medicines won't work. It hits her every time she bends down, and she's got to lie flat on her back for at least thirty minutes to get straight." He looked at Rainbow. "Ain't that so?"

"That's right."

Rainbow leaned back, closed her eyes with a wrinkle of pain and pushed into the small of her back with both hands. Her knees opened up and her legs came apart and reached outward like claws.

"No matter where I'm at or who I'm with, I got to go down." She gave Gerald a painful smile. "Flat on my back till the pain quits," she finished.

Gerald fidgeted a little and he was sweating at the temples. He teetered on the edge of his chair and had to brace himself to keep from falling.

A. J. said: "But that's not mainly why we come."

"It's not?" Gerald gasped.

"No sir, 'fraid not. Rainbow here was born an unlucky child. I know that may be hard for some to believe." Gerald nodded involuntarily. "What I mean is, the girl's got herself a loose eye. It comes on her every time she gets over-excited." He turned to Rainbow. "You think maybe you could show

Reverend Evans what it's like?"

"Go ahead, Rainbow," Leroy said.

Rainbow said she would try. She closed her eyes for a moment and then opened them wide and strained and thought about that $1,500 mink coat. Gerald was fascinated. His eyes opened wide with hers and drank in the fullness of this event as if it were a revelation.

They waited and sure enough in about half a minute Rainbow's right eye started to roll. It was not the kind of roll that came when Rainbow really got worked up over something, but it rolled, and Gerald thought it was terrible and beautiful.

"Don't hurt yourself, Rainbow," A. J. told her and looked at Gerald. "See what I mean? Well, what I was thinking was this. How'd it be if Rainbow started coming to your meetings and listening to you preach? I bet she'd get a lot out of that."

"I done tried everything else," Rainbow said softly, her voice cracking a little.

A. J. and Leroy nodded. A. J. went on: "We wouldn't even mind giving a contribution either, would we Leroy? These people have all kinds of expenses."

Leroy nodded and Gerald smiled. "You're right, son," Gerald said. "We call it the Healing Faith Gospel Gift."

A. J. said: "It'd sure be worth it if you could help fix that clutch and stop that rolling eye." A. J.'s tone was cordial. "And just maybe down at the beauty finals Saturday night after your services up here, you and some of your people might come down and give Rainbow a little moral support. She'd be proud if you did."

Gerald was not a hard man to deal with. "Don't see why not."

A. J. and Gerald looked at each other closely. They were now talking about the same thing and the subject was money. A. J. took out a twenty and a five and laid them on the table. It was a moment of crisis and truth. Gerald glanced at the money and then looked away into the distance, his gaze soulful and visionary. And he said softly, invitingly: "Our men and women and our children will come down to that pageant of beauty and good health and to the aid of a sister for as little a thing as fifty dollars."

A. J. stood up and smiled. He touched the $25 and said as if making a speech to the Rotary, "We couldn't be happier to give twenty-five dollars right now and the rest Saturday night." And he offered Gerald his hand to shake on the deal. Gerald seemed a little surprised. He hesitated a second, before taking A. J.'s hand. Then Rainbow said in her prettiest voice:

"I feel better already."

A. J. and Gerald continued their handshake. They were both smiling now. It was a fine moment. Christian and pagan had met on a hillside above the beautiful White River in Batesville, Arkansas, and a bond of fellowship and mutual interest had sprung up between them. It was a wonderful thing.

The big Carnival Parade started at the bottom of the hill on the north side of Batesville and came up through town and down again and ended at the White River bridge. It rolled in slow spurts and stops, like a mighty caterpillar, one that was gaily decorated and tooting and blaring and moving through a swirl of confetti and fluttering streamers and flags.

There were six bands in the parade and over fifty cars, half of them carrying beauty queens, perched on the back seats of convertibles like birds. Some of the girls rode alone and some with their little sisters or brothers. There were also three floats, twenty-nine horses, and twenty-nine sheriff's deputies with guns on their hips and ranger hats; five policemen on motorcycles, several boat and motor displays pulled on flatbed trucks, the mayor, who rode with the fire chief, the police chief in a patrol car, and Dr. Evans, who walked and carried a Bible.

And there was a troop from the Batesville VFW and American Legion stuffed into their uniforms like potatoes in a sack, a National Guard marching unit from Little Rock in gleaming helmets plus some fifteen or twenty ex-soldiers Molly and them had rounded up from Poinsett County who were sweating and badly in need of a beer. The queen of the parade was Posey "Purple Sage" Trigg, the country singer from Nashville, Tennessee, who rode in the third car with her manager and uncle, Gus Trigg, of Pampa, Texas, where Posey had been born.

Rainbow rode in a yellow Cadillac convertible that belonged to Billy Luke, and her driver was a boy named Cecil Spurrier, whose father owned a gin in Trumann. Cecil was nineteen and had some money, but he was awkward and over-eager. He kept asking Rainbow for a date: for that afternoon or that night or tomorrow or tomorrow night or maybe for breakfast and church on Sunday and he went into next week and the week after and finally asked her for Labor Day.

"I'm busy," Rainbow told him. "Watch what you're doing."

"What about Christmas?" Cecil said. "You can't be busy that far ahead."

"I am. Just keep your eyes on the road, kid. And drive straight—and slow."

It was a fine day for a parade. The sky overhead was an ashen blue from the heat and then descended to the horizon behind an orange haze that hung there like a harem veil. The river was clear and blue-green. It flowed gently. The Corps of Engineers up at Bull Shoals and Norfolk had shut down all but one generator under the dams so the river would be just right. Boys and girls swam out into the middle, kicking and splashing, and others were out in boats waiting for the cars to come down.

There must have been 10,000 people lining the streets. Nearly everyone from Batesville was there and some from as far away as Little Rock and Fort Smith. The street seethed like a cluster of aphids. The kids ducked and crawled between legs and some older boys hung from light poles like telephone men. The river boys who worked commercial fishing boats came to town and they were drinking in the hot sun and drawing scorn and envy.

A. J., Leroy, and Pierpont and all of the members of the Highway 70 Six moved down the street with Rainbow's car, hollering and whooping and jumping to see over the crowd like birddogs in tall grass. Even Doodle Socket was caught up in the spirit of the day, and he walked down the street, his eyes glistening behind his dark glasses, and he gave peanuts and candy to children. With Doodle Socket was Trent Dangerfield, his agent from Memphis, and Trent had worked out something for Doodle to sing on the program Saturday night. Doodle Socket passed out lots of candy. He was feeling fine.

Flossie and Molly and Billy Luke were there and Molly's man, Shade, and a bunch of men from the VFW who weren't marching, and their wives, and every kid who could walk. They all cheered and waved flags and sometimes the men ducked into doorways or alleys to take quick, hot, lip-stinging bites from pints of whiskey.

The parade broke up about two o'clock at the bridge and Rainbow jumped out of the car before Cecil could stop her. She left him standing in the front seat yelling with his hands cupped to his mouth:

"Rainbow! Come back! I want to talk to you about something serious. Come back!" His voice rang out like the kid calling for Shane.

Rainbow found A. J., Molly, and Leroy, and Molly said she wanted to see that $1,500 mink. They had moved the coat from Thorndike's that morning to a boathouse on the river. Doodle Socket and Trent went with them. Trent was a tall, dark man with a low secretive way of talking and had curvy lips. He kept giving Rainbow the eye.

The stage was complete and rested out on the water on pontoons and was anchored with sections of railroad track. It floated alongside the boathouse, which pageant officials used to stage the program and where the girls changed between events. About four hundred chairs had been set up in rows reaching back from the bank and there were places behind for people to sit on the grass. Farther back on the hill was Gerald's revival tent.

The fur coat was locked in a glass case and was still draped over the headless mannequin. Trent said it was worth every bit of $1,500. He said he knew because Boark Purtle, a singer he represented, had bought one just like it last month for his mother, and he had handled the deal. Trent said no one else but Rainbow could come close to doing justice to that mink. Rainbow liked Trent.

149

Later that afternoon, all of Rainbow's supporters, excluding Gerald's group, came up to Doris and Joe's for a party and there were close to seventy-five people there. They brought their own whiskey, but Doris had ice and popcorn. It was pretty noisy for a while and then Rainbow stood up with a glass of Coke (they wouldn't let her drink) and proposed a toast to A. J.

"I owe a lot to the Kid, here," she said and smiled.

"We all do."

"That's right."

"That goes for me, too," Doris said. Everybody clapped.

Pepper had been drinking fast again, and he was a little tight. He stepped forward and proposed his own toast and said:

"I'll tell you what! That son of a bitch could be president if he wanted to."

Then Pepper slipped back and would have fallen if Leroy hadn't caught him.

About six o'clock, a hush fell over the house and porch. A few minutes later, they all started for the river.

The sun was dropping behind the trees on the hills and a light wind dipped down over the water and blew coolly up the bank. A string of lights stretched out over the water to the stage, and the boathouse was lighted and sparkling like a mound of jewels. A. J., Leroy, and Pierpont were in the front row with Flossie and Molly and Shade. Behind them sat the rest of the Highway 70 Six and the other roadhouse people. In a solid block up the aisle sat Gerald and his counselors and followers nearly a hundred strong, though some of them looked very pale or thin and a couple of guys sat with crutches.

Joe and Doris came late, but A. J. had saved them seats next to him. Joe was wearing his conductor's uniform as usual and Doris held his arm. It was 7:30. The moon was out, still pale but turning into a rich gold. A train whistled through the valley and Joe leaned to Doris and said with a smile:

"The 212's on time. Right on time."

Doris' eyes were a little misty.

Molly nudged A. J. "Keep your fingers crossed, Kid."

A. J. grinned and squeezed her arm. Off somewhere a dog was barking. He broke into a long, yapping howl and then the orchestra struck up "Turkey in the Straw."

Creasepool Handley, a fiddler from Mountain View, who was the master of ceremonies, came on stage to a wave of applause and opened the show with a couple of stories. Then he introduced Posey, who sang "I Don't Know When It's Raining 'Cuz I'm in Love With You." The people loved it. Doodle Socket was next with "Rawhide," and he got almost as big a hand as Posey.

The finals in the talent competition for queen of the White River Water Carnival began at eight o'clock sharp.

Emily Ann Thalmueller, Miss Little Red, sang "I'm in Love with a Wonderful Guy," and her voice was clear and strong and beautiful. Emily Ann got a fine round of applause. Miss Crooked Creek, Pauline Dietz from Harrison, did a dance in tights to the theme from Scheherazade, and Pauline got a good hand, too. Miss Perch, Rosemary Bettis from Marshall, came on strong with a tightrope act, and the people loved it when Sarah Bloodworth, Miss Smallmouth Bass from Yellville, did her imitations of a quail, a turtle dove, and a barred owl.

All Rainbow did was twirl her baton and walk around some on the stage. The music they played for her was "Body and Soul," and they played it real slow. Rainbow didn't do anything else; she just walked and twirled and every once in a while she would stand and twirl. And she didn't drop her baton once. She was wearing a spangled and shiny red and white majorette's costume with short pants trimmed in white fur, and people said later she hadn't needed that baton at all.

When she finished with a bow, Gerald was the first one on his feet. He lifted his arms as a signal, and one hundred blushing Christians stood with him and applauded for five minutes. Molly and Flossie and Billy Luke and Shade and all of the VFW boys and their wives and children rose up and swelled the applause. Leroy whistled between his teeth with a sound like a dive bomber. A. J. was up on his chair clapping and stamping like José Greco. Doodle Socket was going through his moves. Even Trent Dangerfield stood up.

As the applause finally began to die, A. J. turned and waved his appreciation at Gerald, and then he looked beyond Gerald to some trees along the bank and then out to some boats waiting in the river. He raised his hand, and on this signal two guys started climbing the trees and the drivers of the boats switched their engines on and let them idle quietly.

Pauline was crying when Rainbow came back to the side of the stage. She was finished and she knew it. Emily Ann looked at Rainbow and her teeth were clenched.

"Where'd all them rooters of yours come from?" she growled.

Rainbow studied her for a moment. "Baton twirling's an art, honey. People go for that."

"Jesus Christ!"

The bathing suit competition came at 9:15, and Rainbow's slow walk, her profile poses and her bow started the same thing over again. Gerald was clapping so hard his hands were red. The tent crowd was still blushing and still applauding. The roadhouse people screamed and whooped, and now the boys in the trees cut loose with sirens and whistles, and out in the boats the drivers honked their horns and kept turning their lights on and off. Even the backers of other queens were applauding. Rainbow's bandwagon was rolling now.

And then, as the five finalists in the 1956 White River Water Carnival and Beauty Pageant stood out on the floating stage in evening dresses and the orchestra played "A Little Bit of Tenderness," the judges voted. At exactly 9:47, when the night was full of stars and the moon looked like a golden bolt shot in the sky, Creasepool announced over the loudspeaker system, which carried the word up and down the river and flying into the hills, that Rainbow Wimberly from Hazen, Arkansas, was the new White River Carnival queen. It was Rainbow's moment of glory.

The applause was sudden and thunderous, like a landslide. The music was loud and jumpy. A. J., Leroy, and the boys of the Highway 70 Six rose to their feet hugging each other and everyone near them, and then they got up on their seats, whistling and shouting. It sounded like a dozen factories letting out at once. Pierpont stood up on his chair, and he was already hoarse from yelling.

Molly and Flossie hugged each other and Doris kissed Joe, who took out a timetable from his inside coat pocket and tore it into hundreds of pieces, letting them fly in the air like confetti. The VFW boys were standing and yelling and their wives and children were either crying or roaring. Everyone of the Christians felt wonderful, including Gerald, who was thinking about that second $25.

Will bent down and pulled up his pants and showed everybody his right sock. "I had it rolled for luck!" he screamed, and then he raised his foot so everyone could see, pointing to it with a half-crazed smile. There is nothing like a totem that works. Then he stepped down to the river and began yodeling furiously and gloriously at the top of his lungs. It scared the frogs for a hundred yards, and out in the middle of the river, an old fish rolled once and then sounded for the deep.

Thurmond and Pepper were dancing and screaming. They stopped their dance and socked each other on the shoulder and then on the chin. Pepper took one a little too hard on the chin and fell right into the arms of Gerald Evans, who held him like a baby.

Cecil and Billy Luke started dancing and kicking like Cossacks, but Billy Luke had to watch his kick on account of that recent hernia. Doodle Socket was on his chair with his thumbs in his belt, his head back and his eyes closed, writhing like a man at the end of a rope. His lips moved and he was singing, but nobody could hear because of the noise. Doodle didn't even have his dark glasses on.

Shade stood up and finally spoke. "Well, I'll be damned," he said and sat back down, cracking his knuckles and grinning like a horse.

A. J. and Leroy jumped out on the stage. They grabbed Rainbow and flung her around and kissed her and Rainbow laughed uproariously. "I done all right, hey?"

A. J. said: "You dang whistling!"

Leroy picked her up and squeezed her as hard as he could.

Rainbow was breathless when he put her down, but she got right to business. "Leroy, I want to put on that mink and I can't wait another minute."

It was about eighty degrees and Leroy said: "Right now?"

Rainbow pinched his chin and gave it a little jerk. "Right now!"

A. J. went with Leroy to get the mink, and Rainbow, the new queen, the star, the center of attention, as it sometimes will happen in moments of tumult and celebration, found herself suddenly alone. It did not take long to fill the gap. Molly and Doris and Joe and Flossie were on their way, Miss Summerall was bearing down on her, her face flashing with smiles like a blinker system, and Creasepool was sidling over.

But Harley Knight got to her first.

Harley was a disk jockey from Batesville, a fast talker with a lean face and a ducktail haircut who wore white bucks and a seersucker suit. Harley took Rainbow by the arm and pointed toward the far side of the stage where he had his equipment set up. Harley said: "Miss Wimberly, would you step this way for an interview? I'm Harley Knight from KBTA."

"Lead the way, darlin'."

There were two chairs beside Harley's recording machine, the kind of chairs that have canvas trip backs. Rainbow settled down and felt just like Lana Turner on a movie set. She stuck out her chest and crossed her legs.

Harley got a level and began: "Well, Miss Wimberly, you're now the new White River Carnival queen. How do you feel?"

"Richer."

Harley laughed and frowned at the same time. "No, I mean it. How do you feel?"

Rainbow gave him a pleasant frown. "I told you that. Wait'll they get back with that ranch mink. You'll see."

Harley checked his notes and tried again. "Now, then, you have also won a one-thousand-dollar prize. I suppose you'll want to use that to further your college education."

"Naw."

"You don't want to further your college education?"

"Don't see it, honey. Been to high school."

Harley tried a little smile but it fell off. "Miss Wimberly, are your mother and father here for your big night?"

"Daddy won't leave Hazen. No use trying."

"What does your father do?"

"Huh?"

"What does your daddy do? What's he do for a living?"

"Oh. He drives a tractor."

"Well, that's interesting. What kind of tractor?"

"Aw, come on, Harley. You see one tractor you seen 'em all. Say, you look pale."

"Do I?"

Rainbow looked at him closely. "I seen more color in a dead bass."

Harley was choking a little now. "Tell us about yourself, Miss Wimberly. About your hobbies. If you have a job?"

Rainbow nodded. "Sure. I'm a nightclub stander."

"A what?"

Rainbow got up and showed him how she did it. "Like so."

Harley said: "You mean you work in a nightclub?" He glanced over at Miss Summerall. She had been listening and was moving in slowly in the stance of a boxer.

Rainbow smiled a shy little smile and sat back down. "Aw, it's not too much. Not what you'd call a regular act. Listen, Harley, while you're thinking up some more questions, mind if I use your mike? Glad you mentioned pa. Want to say hi to him and ma and the kids."

Harley told her to go ahead. "Do you have a large family?"

"Naw. I just got two."

Harley's grip on the microphone tightened, and it really got tight. "You mean YOU have children?"

It had come out so naturally and unexpectedly, but Rainbow knew she was in trouble now. She looked around for A. J. and Leroy. Pepper and Thurmond were standing behind a circle of people, grinding their teeth and shaking their heads like they were holding hot wires. And then Rainbow got mad. Her loose eye started to roll and she said:

"Hell, man! What's wrong with motherhood?" Her eye rolled even more.

Harley said quietly: "You're a married woman? Speak right into the mike."

Rainbow hesitated. "Well, in a manner of speaking. Yeah." Thurmond and Pepper looked at each other in great pain. Miss Summerall had one fist clenched. Creasepool coughed. Leroy and A. J. had come back. They had heard the last part of this. Leroy was holding the coat and thinking how soft it was. A. J. closed his eyes and his chin sank to his chest.

Miss Summerall said: "I'll take that coat! Miss Wimberly is disqualified!" She reached for the coat.

Rainbow jumped up with a snarl. "Oh, no you won't! Come here with that mink!"

Leroy stepped back, and Rainbow and Miss Summerall both had hold of the coat. They pulled and neither would let go. They pulled harder and each rocked with the force of the other's tug. And then Rainbow gave one mighty yank and tore the coat from Miss Summerall's hands and the lining ripped loose with a loud split. Miss Summerall lunged for the coat, and both she and Rainbow, with fistfulls of fur and kicking like cats, fell to the floor. That's how it started.

The word spread to the other girls and to the people on the stage and then leaped from the stage like a brushfire and raced through the crowd. "Miss Wimberly is disqualified!" The murmur grew to a roar, and some of the people who had started home, turned back like spectators at a football game when the tide suddenly turns.

On the stage, Creasepool went to the aid of Miss Summerall. That brought A. J. and Leroy into it. A group of men emerged from the boathouse with their fists clenched and the Highway 70 Six took them on. Police materialized from the shadows, carrying nightsticks. The beauty queens screamed and the mothers and fathers looked around anxiously. Some of the people from Marked Tree and Lepanto were crying. The conductor of the orchestra tried to get the music going, but two violinists and one of the saxophone players were making tracks along the river, keeping to the shadows and trying to hide their instruments.

Out in the seats, Shade stood up. He stared at a few guys, then told everybody to take it easy. A cop came over and told Shade to take it easy himself. Shade sort of backed up and smiled. The cop came at him, raising his billy club, and Shade picked up a wooden chair. It came apart in three pieces when Shade hit him with it, and the cop saw stars.

Nearby, the men from the Marked Tree and Lepanto VFWs gave their pints of whiskey to their wives and looked around for troublemakers. Some Legionnaires from Batesville were looking, too, and so were some of the river boys. They all found each other and the swinging started. Gerald did his best to stop it. He tried, with an urgent and passionate plea, he tried, but was downed with a fine roundhouse from a knot-armed former infantry major, and he fell among the chairs and at the knees of a huddled woman, his ankle twisted beneath him.

On the stage it was wild. People were falling in the water and bottles were flying. Emily Ann tried for a piece of that mink that Rainbow and Miss Summerall were, by now, tearing apart. She missed and tripped and fell into the water. She screamed and struggled wildly. Finally, a policeman reached out his hand and grabbed her. A moment later and it would have been too late. Miss Little Red, bless her soul, couldn't swim a stroke.

Will was sparring with a policeman and trying to keep out of the way of a nightstick. And then Will stopped completely, held up his hand and gave out with a terrible burst of yodeling. The policeman stood speechless and a little scared. Will hit him with a fast right cross, and the cop was out of business.

And the fighting spread. It moved out into the parking places and up the hill and even into the streets of the town. There were automobile crashes and sounds of broken windows and horns and sirens and barking dogs. And the night train shrieked through wailing like a demon. The only thing missing was a thunderstorm.

And then, just before the end, it was never discovered exactly how, a grass fire broke out where the cars had been parked. It spread up the hill, swirling and tossing and merrily crackling in flaming waves toward Gerald's revival tent. The ropes caught and then the flaps, and the sides and the top, and finally the chairs inside were roaring and popping like kindling. The flames reached fifty feet into the air, and you could feel the heat all the way down to the river. But there was some good in this, because the people stopped fighting when they saw the fire.

It was a sad spectacle when it was all over. The strings of lights on the stage were down, and there was not a glimmer from the boathouse. Only one globe was still burning on the edge of the stage, and it shone forlornly next to the water. Fish came up for a look and then drifted away into the darkness. It was very quiet. No sound came from the birds. The dogs had stopped barking. And the river ran silently with barely a whisper.

The mink coat lay worthless and torn on the stage, parts of it scattered around like scalps. Police with flashlights prowled through the broken seats and along the river looking for the injured. The fire was finally out and firemen poked through the ashes. Gerald sat under an elm tree below the ruins, shaking desperately. His tent was gone but his trailer and truck had been saved. After a while he got up and moved off into the night. He limped as he walked. It was to prove a permanent thing and, as it turned out, bad for business.

They arrested close to fifty people that night. A. J., Leroy, and the other members of the band spent the night in jail, as did Flossie and Molly and Billy Luke and Cecil and Shade. Nobody slept it was so crowded. Only Pierpont, Doris, and Joe made it back home. Pierpont had his hands full calming both of them down and had to give Joe a pint of whiskey to make him sleep. Rainbow spent the night in the chief's office alternately sobbing and cursing over the world's shortest reign as a beauty queen.

The next day, about noon, at City Hall in a ceremony that nearly went unnoticed, Emily Ann Thalmueller of Greers

Ferry, sniffling and suffering from a bad cold, was named carnival queen. She received her $1,000 check, but there was no mink coat that year.

The Batesville mayor wanted to keep everybody in jail for a week. "Look at what they did down there," he said to Police Chief Teddy Street. "I haven't seen anything like that since the war."

But Teddy said no because it would cost too much to feed everybody, and he didn't want to put up with it anyhow, so he kept the people in jail on Sunday and charged them a $20 fine then started turning them loose on Monday morning. It took some time to complete the paperwork and for people to get their possessions back, and it was after noon before A. J., Rainbow, and the others got back to Doris and Joe's.

They didn't stay long, just long enough to ice down a tub of beer which they put in the back of A. J.'s pickup along with Pete's horse, Sonny, and a couple of bales of hay. They said good-bye to Doris and Joe and took off. Leroy, Rainbow, and the boys drove behind A. J. and Pierpont, and Doodle Socket brought up the rear. On the hill across the river, the little caravan pulled to a stop and everybody got out and had a beer.

Down along the river, smoke was still rising from the ashes of Gerald's tent, and an acrid smell hung in the air. At the boat dock some men were stacking the chairs and tearing down what was left of the stage. A short distance from the river in an open field, Gerald, who had seen trouble before, was getting ready for the final services of his revival, which had been postponed on Sunday because of the trouble. The musicians were tuning up and some of the people were singing, loudly, but a little off key.

Rainbow and the others were feeling pretty low. The beer helped, but it was just something to do, there was no real pleasure in drinking it. A. J. was worried. A couple of times he started to say something funny, tell a joke and make light of the whole thing. After all, nobody had died, and nobody owed anybody any money and Sonny, after all, was safe and had his bales of hay, and the beer was cold even if it wasn't all that satisfying. But A. J. couldn't bring himself to do it.

He could look around at the faces. Leroy had his head down, frowning like he was overdrawn at the bank; Rainbow's chin was stuck out defiantly; she was glaring at everybody, and once A. J. thought he saw her eye start to roll. Doodle Socket had that smirk on his face as if to say what was a star doing out here with a bunch of nobodies, but it was hard to tell who or what he was mad at exactly because he kept muttering what a son of a bitch Ed Sullivan was. Pepper was over by Leroy's Ford and would occasionally sneak a look at his acne in the sideview mirror and make a face like he was dying. Will didn't seem to be concerned about anything. He was over to one side as usual yodeling quietly, but it was sad yodeling. Pierpont was edgy and kept looking at A. J.

At last, Thurmond crushed a beer can in his hand like it was a paper cup, pitched it away and said: "Well, shit, I think I'll get some of that screwdaddle myself and really get with it."

That's when A. J. said, "Naw, hell, let's get on over to the Silver Moon and see what's cooking. What this bunch needs is some hot lick music and a lot to drink."

"You sure about that, Kid?" Pierpont said.

They all stood up kind of slow and everybody got a fresh, cold can of beer and then climbed in the cars. Pierpont rode with A. J., and Doodle drove alone as usual. They didn't notice, as they drove away, a shiny Cadillac pull out onto the highway from a side road. It was as black and sleek as a king snake, and Trent Dangerfield was behind the wheel.

Nobody said much on the way over to Newport. In Leroy's car, Pepper and Thurmond sat in the back with Will, and once Leroy asked Will to stop yodeling. Will said he was just about through, yodeled a few more Ah-de-lay-he-has, and quit and said nothing the rest of the way. Rainbow was in the front with Leroy, pushed up against the door as far away from Leroy as she could get with her legs coiled under her and the tips of her high-heeled shoes seemingly aimed right at Leroy's eyes. Leroy noticed the tips and kept quiet.

They stopped at the first liquor store across the Jackson County line, and they were all feeling a little better when they got to the Silver Moon. But it wasn't what you'd call a wedding day atmosphere, not even close.

Doodle Socket pulled into the parking lot, spitting out of the window as was his custom at the Silver Moon. Leroy and A. J., who'd got behind Doodle at the liquor store, pulled in beside him. They all sat there a few moments and took deep breaths and some straight whiskey before going in. A few minutes later, Trent drove up, parked his Cadillac over next to A. J.'s pickup, and went inside. He sat at the bar unnoticed and didn't say anything.

It was pretty quiet for the Silver Moon. The place was about half filled. On Mondays there was no band, but the jukebox was going: Bobby Pickett, singing "The Love Sick Blues."

Doodle Socket set the tone.

"Never did like this place. Stinks of Elvis." And he looked around just in case Elvis might be there and be dumb enough to say something smart and get his block knocked off.

A. J. was uneasy. There had been fights before and all kinds of trouble in the band, but A. J. sensed that something was different now. All good things had to end, but for that to happen everybody had to agree it was time. You could have a dissenter now and then and a guy who made a fool of himself or was a natural-born fool and things would still be all right. But when there was a general consensus that it was time to split up and move on, that was the end of it, and A. J. had this dismal feeling that soon it would all be over. Now, they were all drinking too fast and talking way too loud and A. J. didn't like it.

Then Leroy said it:

"Rainbow, you and that radio guy. That was really dumb. I mean it was moron-dumb."

"You lay off me, Leroy. I'm warning you!"

"Take it easy, Leroy," A. J. said.

"Give her hell, Leroy," Doodle Socket said. "She's got it coming."

"Shut up, Doodle Socket," Will said.

"Who you tellin' to shut up, two-bit yodeler!"

Will had a look on his face like when he went after Buster Leach with that bicycle chain. A. J. put his hand on Will's shoulder—easy, Will, easy—but he was looking at Rainbow and Leroy.

"Come on now," he said, "let's all settle down."

But Leroy was relentless.

"Like I said, dumb. I could build a bank out of your mental blocks, Rainbow."

"Don't you say *another word* to me!" Rainbow was shouting.

Leroy snorted. He poured some more whiskey into his glass of beer and looked over toward the bar. That's when he saw Trent. Trent had turned around now and was facing them. Leroy said:

"Well, lookee there, Rainbow. If it ain't the old bloodhound Trent. Follows you around like a goat follows a cottonseed wagon, don't he?" Leroy's tone was real snide.

Rainbow turned and waved at Trent. "Well, so it is. Just in time, too." She swung out her legs and shot out her chest. "I think me and old Trent'll cut out of here and have us a little fun."

"No you ain't!" Leroy said and grabbed her arm.

"You get your hands off me. You don't own me. None of you own me!" She was standing now. Her fists were clenched and she was spitting her words. Her eyes switched from Leroy to A. J., back and forth. "You all thought you did. Flipped for me, huh?" she said to A. J. "Flipped a goddam coin! The two big buddies. Big spenders. Big time. Big deal. You're a bunch of sons a bitches, that's what you are!" She reached into her purse, fumbled a moment, and threw a quarter on the table.

"Go on," she said. "Flip it. I dare you!"

A. J. got up. He was placating, easygoing. "Aw, hell, Rainbow, come on. Sit back down here. It ain't all that serious." He put his hands gently on her shoulders.

But she jerked back and slapped him hard on the face.

There was not a sound in the room. Everybody was looking at them: the row of men at the bar, the people at the tables. Trent had turned away slightly but was keeping an eye on Rainbow. The bartender was polishing a glass rapidly when it slipped from his grasp and shattered on the floor.

"God amighty," Will said softly.

Rainbow turned and started for the bar, swaying her hips like a swinging bridge, smoothing down her skirt and letting her legs cut like a pair of scissors across the dance floor. Even after what had happened, everybody later agreed that it was one of Rainbow's best walks. She got to the bar, kissed Trent on the cheek very close to the mouth, and offered him her arm. He took it, and together they started out. At the door, Rainbow stopped and looked back at the boys' table.

"See you," she said and she was gone.

Somebody put a nickel in the juke and the music came on. Over at the table, Doodle Socket said:

"Well, to hell with it. I'm cuttin' out, too. I got better things to do." Then he looked at Will. "I didn't mean that, Will, about your yodeling."

"That's all right. I'd forgot about it."

"Well, see you guys."

"Yeah, Doodle Socket, take it easy."

"Take care."

They ordered some more beer and then Pepper said, "If I'm ever going to own me a drugstore, I reckon it's time I got with it. I got a hell of a lot of learning to do and this rat race ain't taking me no place."

"I'm ready to go," Will said.

"Me, too," said Thurmond.

Leroy looked at A. J. and Pierpont. "I guess we'll be riding on down the pike, Kid." Then he grinned. "I guess I just ain't one of them kind of guys that can keep a band."

"You did all right, Leroy," A. J. said. "You did fine."

Leroy said: "It was nice knowing you, Pierpont. You look after the Kid here. Keep him out of trouble and don't take any wooden nickels yourself, college man."

"I will do my best, but quite often it is not good enough."

163

Leroy winked at him and shook his hand. The others shook Pierpont's hand, then Leroy looked at A. J.

"Well, take it easy, Kid. Keep in touch."

"Yeah. You too." And they left.

A. J. and Pierpont sat at the table sipping their drinks. After a while, they got up and started for the door. But one of the guys at the tables came over and spoke to A. J.

"Hey, man, ain't you the one they call the Watermelon Kid?"

"Some do, yeah."

"We met, remember? Name's Speed Washburn. Back in '48 or was it '47."

"You do look a little familiar."

"Sure. It was over there in Batesville at that watermelon eating contest. You and that fella Jimmy something or other. You sure can eat a lot of watermelon, Kid, hold it, too, as I remember. I won big on you that night. Speaking of that day reminds me, you hear about the carnival over there on the weekend? Saturday night? Tore the place up. Arrested two or three hundred people. Can you believe it?"

"Yeah, I do."

Speed punched A. J. on the arm and said, "Good seein' you again, Kid. Real good."

"Thanks."

Outside, it was just about dark. A. J. and Pierpont stopped by the door, and Pierpont said:

"I'm ready to go home. And I do not lie when I say I could sleep for a week. OK, Kid?"

"Oh, I don't know." A. J. pulled a newspaper clipping from his pocket. "I ran across this the other day. It's about a guy up there north of Berry City. Little place called Grass Valley. Seems he's crazy about planting trees. Hates lumberjacks and sawmills with a passion. Can't stand to see a tree cut. Well, he's gone and got himself in big trouble with the lumber people on account of his thinking on the subject. I'd sure like to meet that scudder."

Pierpont sighed. He looked out toward the open road and back toward the Silver Moon. He shook his head. "Well, I could not let you go alone."

Inside the Silver Moon, the jukebox was going again and they could hear the music. It was Bobby Pickett singing "The Love Sick Blues."

> I've grown so used to you, somehow,
> I ain't nobody's sugar daddy now,
> And I'm oh, so lonesome.
> I got the love sick blues.

All that was twenty years ago. Later I heard how everybody made out. About a year after Newport, Trent got Doodle Socket a contract to appear in a sand and tan movie with Shelley Fabares, but the movie flopped and they soon forgot about that short singer from somewhere in Arkansas. He later got regular work with Gerald's revival group and then moved on up to the Oral Roberts Crusade. He now lives in Tulsa where he is a music instructor at the Oral Roberts University. Doodle drives an LTD, has two little girls, a wife, and a swimming pool in his back yard. Doodle has done all right.

Rainbow married Trent in 1957 and they moved to Los Angeles. But her loose eye kept her out of the picture business after it went wild on her during a screen test with Robert Taylor. She and Trent got divorced right after that. She is married now to a Shell station operator in Fresno, California, and Lester and Clint are living out there. Rainbow is also the mother of three other kids by the Shell guy, and they are all boys. Well, there never could be another Rainbow.

Pepper finally did what he said he was going to. He went back to school to study pharmacology. He now owns a drugstore in Clarendon, and he's doing all right. Thurmond is an MFA insurance agent in Piggott and lives with his mother, who has never gotten any better.

Leroy and Will have stayed together and now have a group called "The Sage Grass." Their music is mostly country-western and some rock. The roadhouse circuit is dead these days. Most of the old places are boarded up or have been torn down, and shopping centers are there now. The farm labor population isn't what it used to be and a lot of little towns have died because the interstates passed them by. The action is in the cities and that's where you'll find Leroy and Will,

Leroy on the piano, and Will on guitar, though Will still does a little yodeling once in a while.

As for A. J., he is married to Betty Sue Runyon from Calf's Neck, whom he met when he and Leroy had been over in the Fourche River country hunting ducks with Will. They'd got hit by an ice storm and had spent the night at Claude Runyon's place. Claude was a friend of Will's and had set up the hunt. A. J. and Betty Sue were married in Perryville in 1959 and they've got a kid named Bobby who is 14. Most people call A. J. Mr. Poole now.

Pierpont never went back to Ohio. He did finally get up to Marshall, though, to see his cousin Ned and his wife, Pearl. But Ned had just pulled out of town, heading for Texas, after going broke in chicken feed. Pierpont lives in DeValls and runs A. J.'s restaurant. DeValls is eight miles off the interstate and business is marginal, but they get by. Alvin is a civil rights lawyer in Little Rock. He drives a black Lincoln Continental, lives in a mixed neighborhood, and makes, so they say, $30,000 a year. Larry Apple still helps A. J. at the boat dock, and there have been no more robberies.

A. J. says he has no complaints. But every once in a while, he'll see an item in the paper about a guy being down on his luck, or he'll get a call from Leroy or Will and something will be wrong, and he'll get up and prowl the house. Sometimes, he'll stand there looking out of the window and his feet will go to tapping. If you don't watch him close, he'll be gone before you know it.